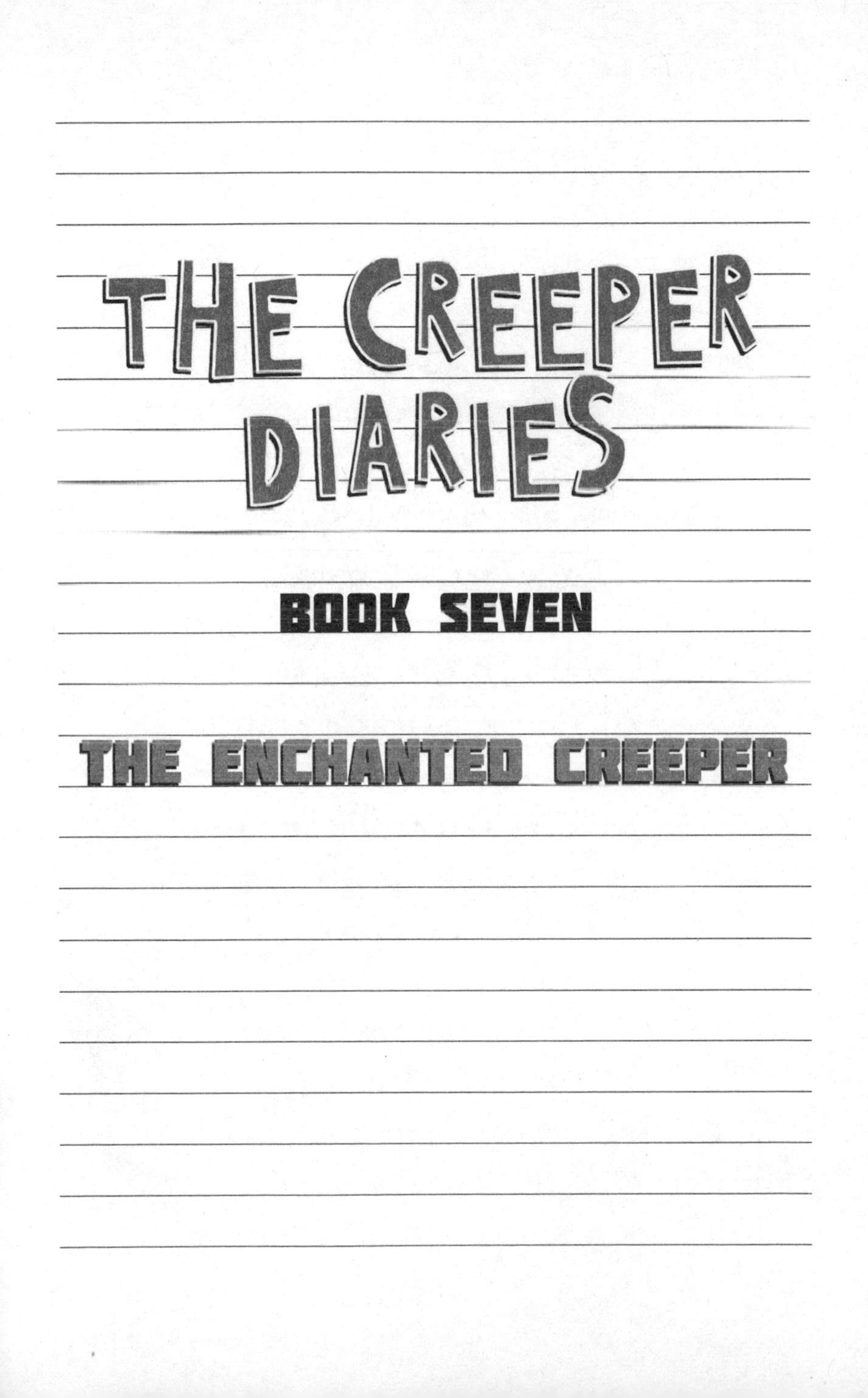
THE CREEPER DIARIES
BOOK SEVEN
THE ENCHANTED CREEPER

Also by Greyson Mann

The Creeper Diaries

Mob School Survivor

Creeper's Got Talent

Creepin' Through the Snow: Special Edition

New Creep at School

The Overworld Games

Creeper Family Vacation

Creeper on the Case

Secrets of an Overworld Survivor

Lost in the Jungle

When Lava Strikes

Wolves vs. Zombies

Never Say Nether

The Witch's Warning

Journey to the End

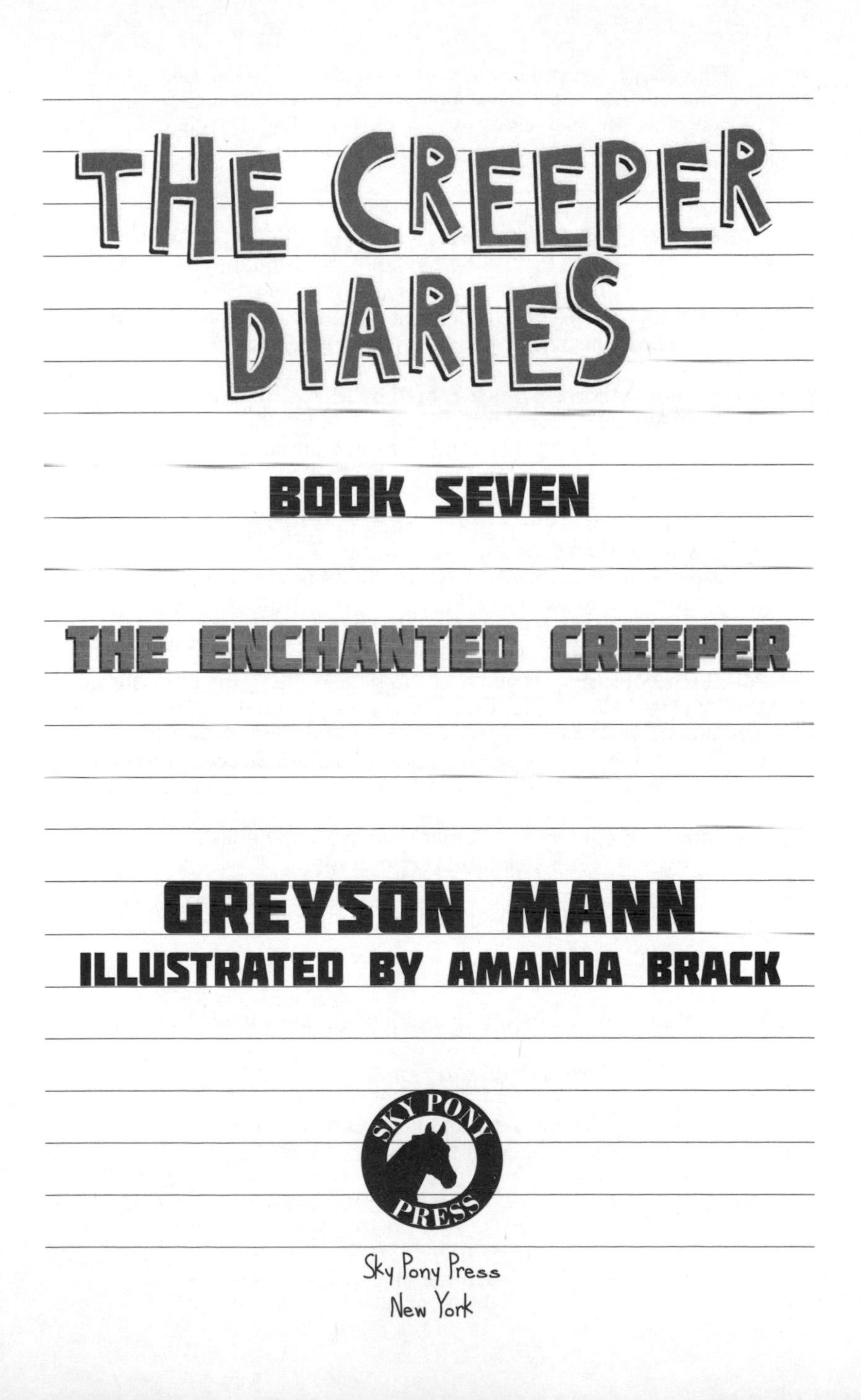

THE CREEPER DIARIES

BOOK SEVEN

THE ENCHANTED CREEPER

GREYSON MANN
ILLUSTRATED BY AMANDA BRACK

SKY PONY PRESS

Sky Pony Press
New York

This book is not authorized or sponsored by Microsoft Corp., Mojang AB, Notch Development AB or Scholastic Inc., or any other person or entity owning or controlling rights in the Minecraft name, trademark, or copyrights.

Sky Pony Press books may be purchased in bulk at special discounts for sales promotion, corporate gifts, fund-raising, or educational purposes. Special editions can also be created to specifications. For details, contact the Special Sales Department, Sky Pony Press, 307 West 36th Street, 11th Floor, New York, NY 10018 or info@skyhorsepublishing.com.

Visit our website at www.skyponypress.com.

10 9 8 7 6 5 4 3 2 1

Library of Congress Cataloging-in-Publication Data is available on file.

Special thanks to Erin L. Falligant.

Cover illustration by Amanda Brack
Cover design by Brian Peterson

Hardcover ISBN: 978-1-5107-3750-1
E-book ISBN: 978-1-5107-3754-9

Printed in the United States of America

DAY 1: THURSDAY

You know how grown-ups are really good at taking something FUN and making it feel like WORK?

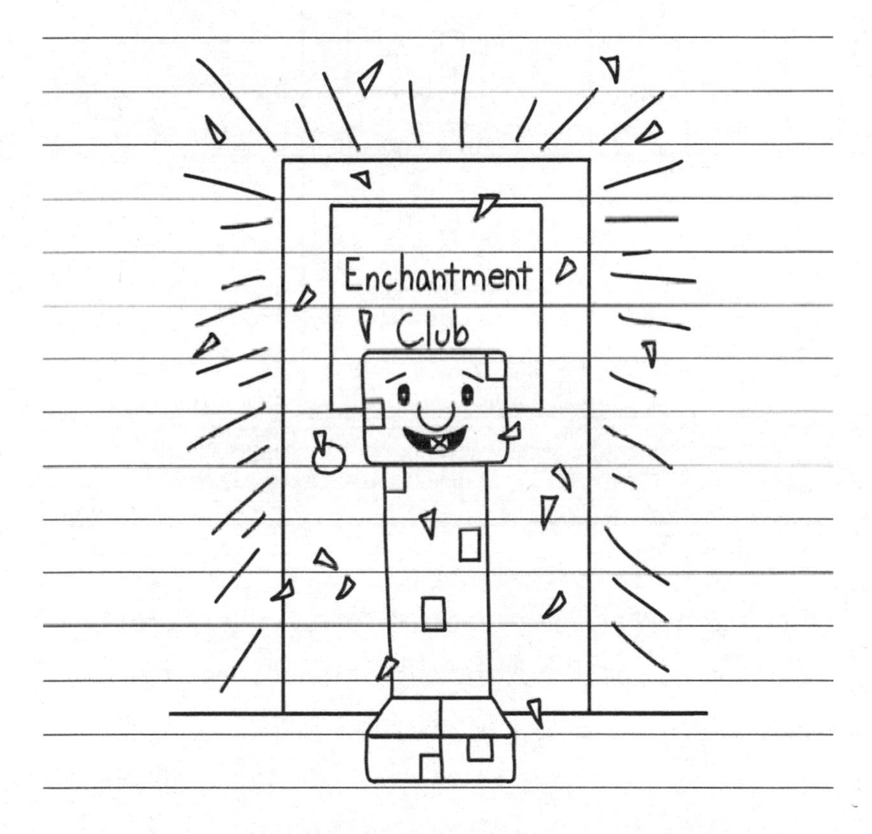

Well, *that's* what happened with the Enchantment Club. It was SUPPOSED to be a club, anyway. But it turned into a CLASS. With homework. And quizzes. And stacks and stacks of books.

I'll tell you what—our teacher, Mrs. Collins, pretty much sucked the fun right out of enchantments. I mean, the quizzes she gives are TOUGH.

What's the difference between the Punch and the Knockback enchantments? How can you get the Frost Walker? Which enchantment works with a sword—Fire Aspect or Flame? Gosh, I don't know,

Mrs. Collins—*that's* a real head-scratcher. I'll have to get back to you on that one.

And here's the real kicker: you can't even CHOOSE which enchantment you get on something. It comes down to pure dumb luck. And my luck really stinks lately.

We started the week by enchanting tools. Me and my buddy Sam Slime brought in pickaxes from home. Sam's looked shiny and new, but mine looked like something Sam's cat had dragged in from the swamp next door.

See, Dad gets really attached to his tools—like they're his precious babies or something. Even though this pickaxe has a dull, wobbly head and the paint is chipping off the handle, Dad could barely part with it. He made me PROMISE to take good care of it and bring it home in one piece. Okay, Dad. Whatevs.

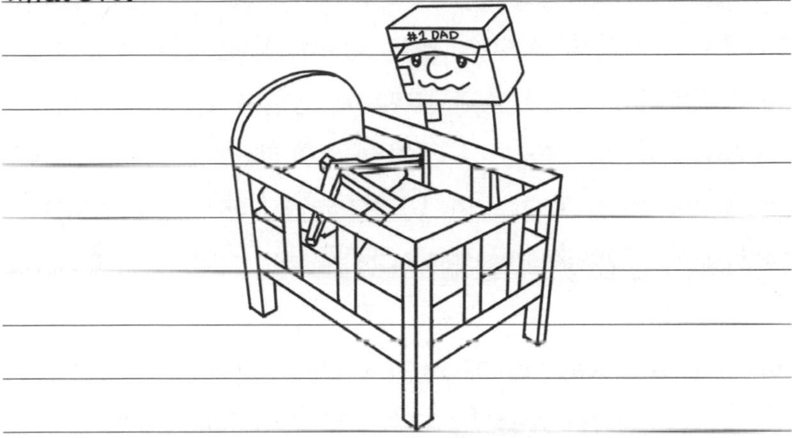

But when it was my turn at the enchantment table, I forgot all about how old that pickaxe was. I put it in the slot on the side of the table, then I dropped a piece of lapis lazuli in the other slot.

Mrs. Collins only lets us use ONE piece of lapis lazuli. There's room for up to three, and I've heard that the more you use, the more enchantments you get—or something like that. But apparently the school budget is pretty tight, so . . . I dropped in my one lousy piece and tried to be grateful. (Mom says I should practice that, since Thanksgiving is coming and all.)

Anyway, this thick book with a gold cover sits on the table, and as soon as I put a chunk of lapis in the slot, the pages of the book started fluttering. Sparks began to fly, and my heart thudded in my green creeper chest. I felt like a witch brewing potions—all powerful like. Which enchantment would I get?

Sam had already gotten the Fortune enchantment for his pickaxe. If he mines with it, he can get WAY more diamonds and emeralds than usual.

And his girlfriend, Willow Witch? She got Silk Touch. She's pretty excited about that, because she can mine more glass for her potion bottles. (Witches are really into that sort of thing.)

When it was my turn, I crossed my toes, hoping for the Fortune enchantment. I could see it in my mind—

the diamonds and emeralds practically LEAPING off cave walls and right into my backpack.

But I didn't get Fortune. You know what I got instead? Unbreaking. GREAT. That means Dad's wobbly old pickaxe will never break. He can keep it forever. Dad will be THRILLED.

I wanted a do-over. But the thing with enchantments is, you pretty much get what you get. There are no second chances. It's like Life sticking out its tongue at you and going "Neener-neener-neener!"

And you know what made things worse? Sam said he wasn't even going to USE his Fortune enchantment for diamonds and emeralds. No sirree. He was going to use it to collect more MUSHROOMS. To make mushroom stew. To share with his cat, Moo.

REALLY???

The only mob in the room who seemed more disappointed than me was Bones. That skeleton LOVES to poke fun at other mobs with his bony fingers and his gang of spider jockeys. He pretty much made my life miserable last year, when I first started Mob Middle School.

But here in Enchantment Class, the ONLY thing Bones wants to enchant is his bow. That dude is all about his bow and arrows. But Mrs. Collins slid her little glasses down on her nose and said that we aren't learning how to enchant weapons and armor "just yet." We'll be sticking with tools for another week.

I caught Bones mocking her behind her back, just to impress his spider jockey friends. But for once, I couldn't blame him. I mean, another week of TOOLS? That meant I was going to need a lot more of them from home. (And Dad was going to have to learn to share.)

I made the mistake of asking Mom for help when I got home. And when she heard I needed to collect old tools for school, she kicked it into high gear. Mom can get a TAD carried away with things like this.

She said it'd be great to clear some clutter out of the house, especially since Aunt Constance is coming for Thanksgiving. Mom is always trying to impress her big sister. It's like this competition thing. Who can knit the longest scarf? Whose house is the tidiest? Whose children are the best behaved? (Mom usually loses on that one. I mean, I'M a pretty decent kid, but I can't speak for my three sisters.)

Now Mom is on a MISSION to cut clutter. She started with the gardening tools she keeps in the chicken coop. Then she decided to clear out some of the chickens, too. Yup, that's right—we have a whole coop full of chickens in our backyard, plus a sheep named Sock. (Don't ask. That's a whole other story.)

Mom decided those chickens would be happier back at the farm where she got them. When she started eyeing up Sock the Sheep, like she was going to send him back too, my baby sister started bawling. Cammy LOVES Sock. And when Cammy doesn't get her way, she blows sky high. (That's why we call her the Exploding Baby.)

So Sock gets to stay, at least for now. But I'm starting to think I'll have to hide my pet squid, Sticky.

Then Mom came in and started cutting clutter INSIDE. She filled a gazillion boxes with stuff to donate to the Creeper Charity. (I guess they send things to homeless mobs in the Nether or something.) Blankets, books, toys—you name it. If it wasn't nailed to the floor, Mom stuffed it into a box. She took a couch pillow right from under my head!

"Less is more," she keeps saying. "You kids don't need all this stuff. You can share."

Yeah, RIGHT. Cammy hasn't really learned how to share yet. And my Evil Twin, Chloe? Nope—she'd rather burn her things than share them with me.

The only sibling I have who SOMETIMES shares is my big sister, Cate. We call her the Fashion Queen because she has a closet full of clothes and costumes. When I needed a rapper costume for the talent show last fall, she hooked me right up.

I can tell Mom is ITCHING to get into Cate's closet and clean it out, but I'm hoping she holds off. See, there might be some leather armor in there that I can use in Enchantment Class. So if Cate has to chain herself to her closet door to keep Mom out, I might have to join her.

The other part of the house Mom can't get into yet is Dad's garage. He told Mom he's working in there, helping Chloe with her science fair project. "Official school business," he told Mom. "It's top secret."

Well, I happen to know EXACTLY what Chloe's project is. It's a dispenser made out of cobblestone that shoots fire charges—mini fireballs, like blasts shoot in the Nether. How do I know, you ask? Because every time I'm in the yard, Chloe tests it out on ME. She aims that dispenser right at me and zings me with fireballs.

Sometimes, I get a warning. I hear the click of the dispenser or see the puff of smoke. I try to dive out of the way, but those fireballs are FAST. Before I can hit the ground, one pings me in the back of the head or bounces off my butt. And Chloe laughs her creeper head off.

The worst part is, I haven't come up with a science fair project of my own. I mean, any mob who knows me KNOWS I'm not a fan of science. Math? Sure. Art? Yup. But science? Not so much.

Still, I have to come up with SOMETHING. Partly because my life's mission is to beat my Evil Twin EVERY chance I get. And partly because of the prize.

See, last year, the winner of the science fair got a bag full of emeralds, and you know what she did with it? Bought a jukebox. Yup, I heard it with my very own ears from my buddy Eddy Enderman. Her own personal jukebox. If I *had that* in MY room? I could listen to Kid Z's *rap* songs ALL night long.

So every *time* Chloe zings me with a fireball, I remind *myself that* I'm *going to* zing *her right* back—by winning *the* fair. And I *have* a BIG advantage: Chloe doesn't *take* Enchantment Class till next semester. So I'm *thinking* I can use enchantments to make a killer science fair project—one that will blow Chloe's dispenser right out of the water (er, I mean the garage).

The only problem is, I don't have a SINGLE idea for a project. And with the homework from Enchantment Class, plus my regular homework, plus all the work it takes to stay out of Mom's way (so that she doesn't find me standing still and donate ME to some charity), I don't really have time to come up with a science project.

I'd almost given up—until school last night. We were in Enchantment Class, and Willow Witch was bummed out about the enchantment she got for her shears. "Potions are WAY better than enchantments," she said. "At least with potions, you can choose which one you want to brew."

I agreed with her. (And let me tell you, THAT doesn't happen very often.) But so far, I'd been getting pretty lame enchantments, too.

Well, Mrs. Collins overheard us and said that you CAN choose which enchantments you give to things.

HUH?

Sure, she said. You do it by enchanting books. Books let you save enchantments for later. Then you can use something called an anvil to transfer those enchantments from books to other things.

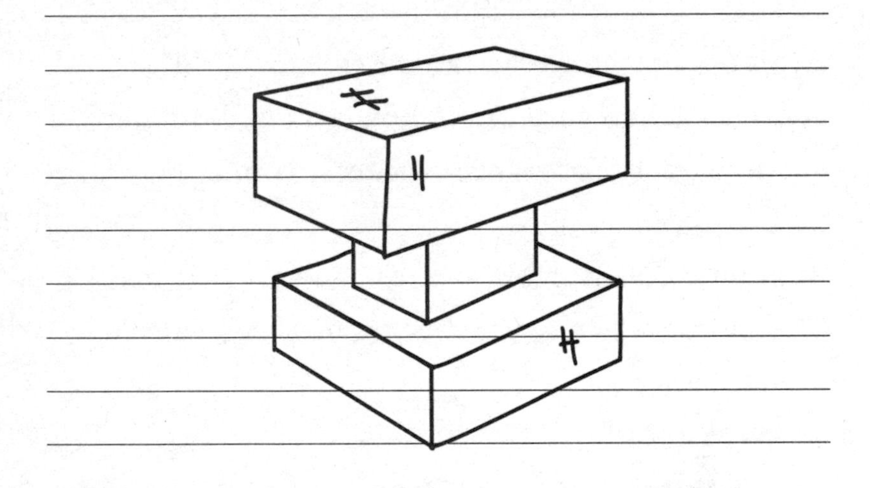

She pointed to this big black anvil in the corner of the enchantment room.

Well, I just about fell off my chair. We've been enchanting for almost a week. So WHEN was Mrs. Collins going to get around to teaching us how to use *that* anvil? I asked *her that*—as *politely* as I could.

And *she* said, "Later. When you're ready."

LATER? *An* anvil isn't *going to help* me LATER. I *have to* come *up* with a science *project* NOW.

I *took* another look at *the* anvil. *That hunk* of iron reminded me of *something* I'd seen in Dad's garage. See, *he got this pile* of iron ingots after a golem was destroyed in a nearby village—destroyed because of a "creeper incident," Dad *told* me. And yeah, he sounded kind of proud about that. (Iron golems and creepers don't really get along.) Dad kept the iron because he thought he could make something out of it someday. He can build pretty much anything.

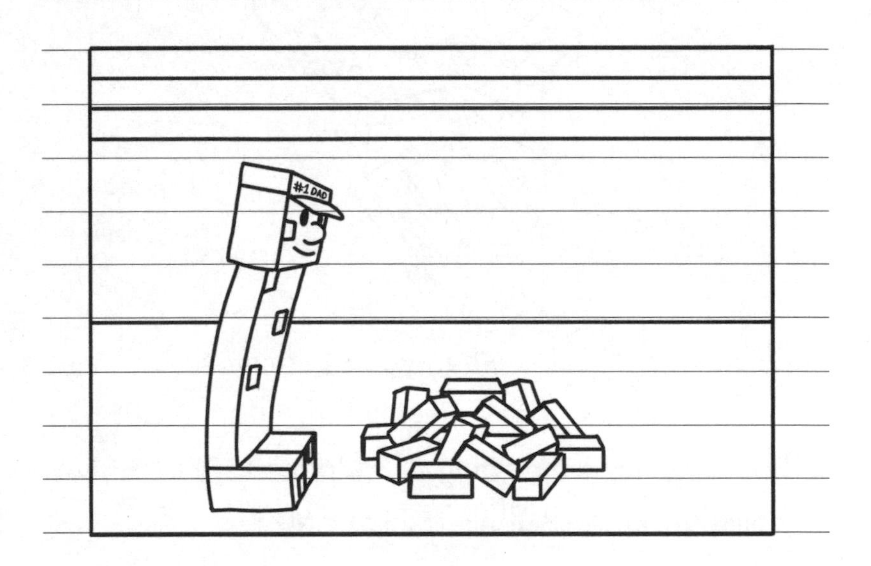

So now I'm home from school, and I'm thinking that "someday" might be TODAY. Dad has enough iron to build an anvil. And I NEED an anvil. Can I convince him to help me build one? Maybe—if I make a plan.

The science fair is at the end of the month, so . . . here's what I'm thinking:

30-Day Plan to a Stellar Science Project

- Convince Dad to help me build an anvil.
- Use enchanted books to come up with an AWESOME science project.
- Burn Chloe with my project—and take home enough emeralds to buy a jukebox!
- Oh, and avoid Mom (before she donates me and everything I love to charity)

I'll start in on Dad tonight, after a good day's sleep. ("Creepers need their sleepers," Dad always says.)

And by the weekend? Dad and I will be pounding iron, side by side, out in the garage. I'm telling you, Chloe and her fire-spitting dispenser don't stand a chance.

DAY 2: FRIDAY

Turns out, convincing Dad to help with the anvil wasn't hard AT ALL. See, after I told Mom that the anvil was part of my science project, she HAD to let Dad keep his huge pile of iron ingots—and all kinds of other crud in the garage that he says he needs for the project.

Dad looked so relieved, a trickle of sweat ran down his creeper face. He went out to the garage before dinner last night and started banging away on that iron. But Mom made me stay inside and finish my homework. I guess she picked up my backpack to move it to "its proper place" and felt how heavy it was.

So I banged out my math homework. Then I read my history chapter. Then I studied all of the enchantments that start with F. I decided to save my science reading for last, because . . . well, you know. Why do NOW what you can put off till later?

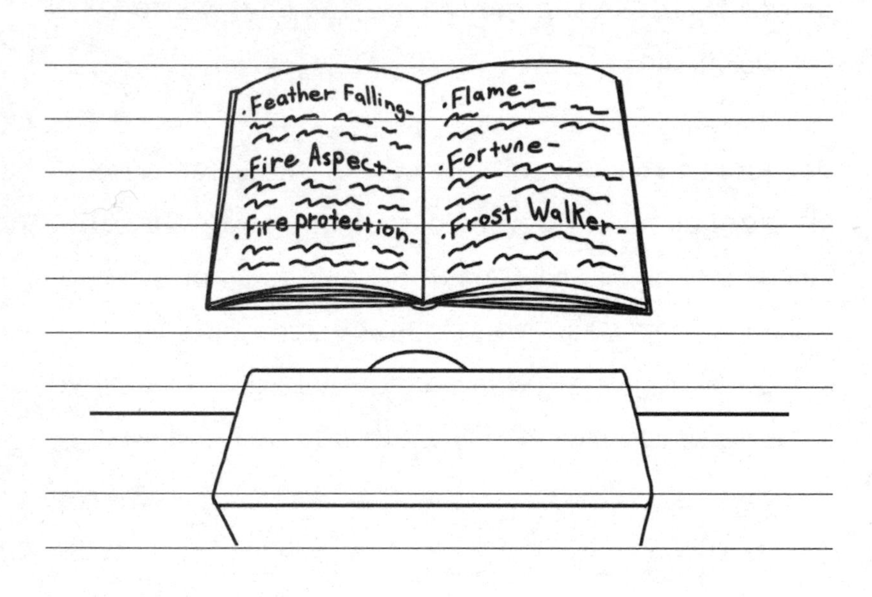

That left just one thing: my Language Arts essay. We have to write two of them a week, which is a LOT. But our new teacher lets me write RAP songs instead of essays. She's a fan of all kinds of writing, she says. FINALLY—a grown-up who gets me!

So I wrote to the sound of Dad pounding on that anvil. Then, after I'd put the finishing touches on my genius rap, I went out to check on Dad's progress.

That's when I ran into Chloe.

If you're wondering how Chloe feels about Dad helping me with my anvil, I'll tell you. She's thrilled about it.

Why? Because every time I walk out to the garage, she zings me with a freakishly fast fireball.

Click! Puff! Zing! (Ouch!)

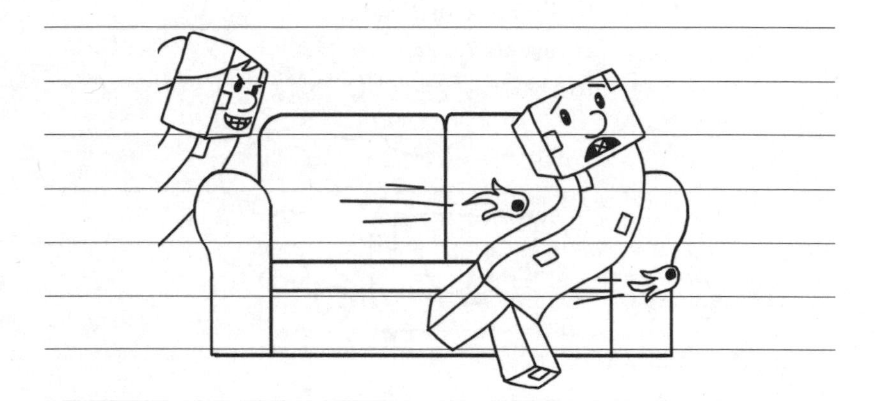

Click! Puff! Zing! (Ouch!)

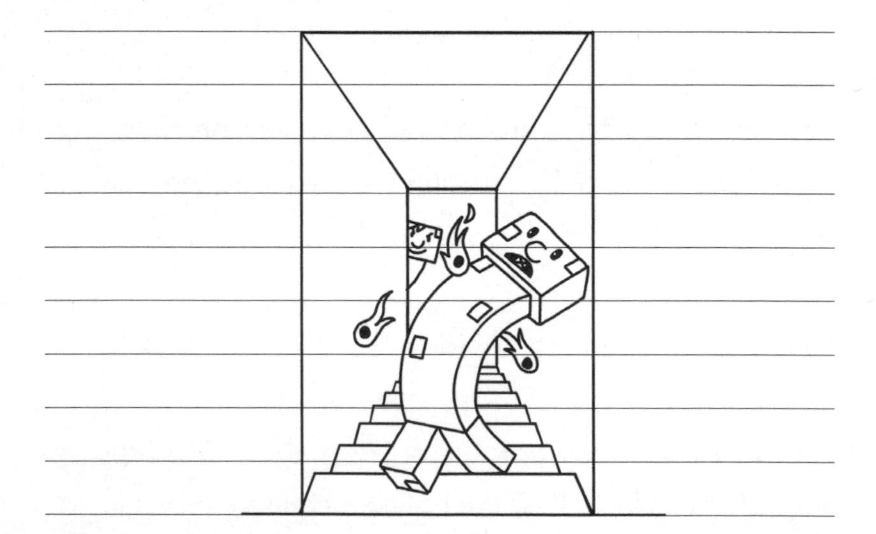

Click! Puff! Zing! (Ouch!)

Yup. EVERY. SINGLE. TIME.

I actually have little green welts on my skin. I even scratched one to make it bigger, so I could run crying to Mom and rat out Chloe.

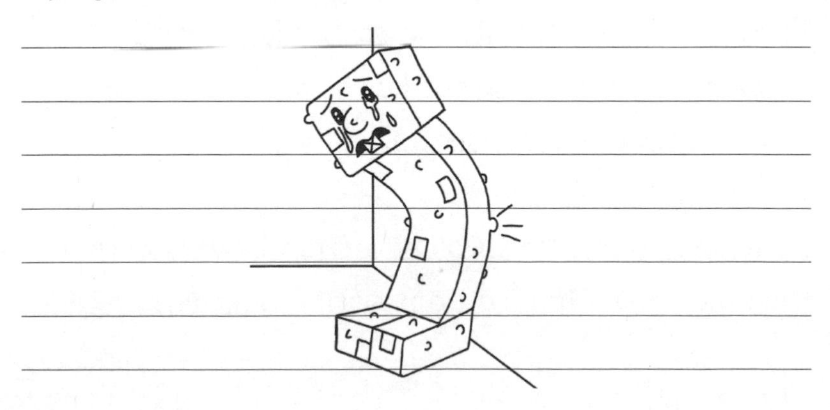

But then I remembered I had my own "on the sly" thing going on with the anvil, so I decided to leave Mom out of it.

Besides, I had work to do! (No, not my science homework. I was hoping that would somehow do itself.) I had to figure out how to enchant a few books so that by the time Dad finished the anvil, I could start USING the thing.

But would Mrs. Collins let me enchant a book in class? Or would she just slide those little glasses down on her nose and say, "LATER, Gerald. You're not ready."

ARGH.

I made a plan on the way to school last night. Enchantment Class is after lunch, but I wasn't going to wait that long. No, sirree.

I decided to pay Mrs. Collins a friendly visit during the lunch hour. It sure beat sitting next to Ziggy

Zombie, who was going on and ON about his science project. It has something to do with blisters and rashes. He actually pulled off his running shoes to show me the other day. "If I run a mile WITHOUT socks, I get THIS kind of blister," he said proudly. "But if I run TWO miles . . ."

Well, last night, I didn't stick around to see those blisters. I took a run of my own—right down to the library. See, the library and the enchantment classroom are next door to each other. And Mrs. Collins usually hangs out in the library. So I wandered in, all whistling and stuff, *pretending* I was just looking for a good book to read.

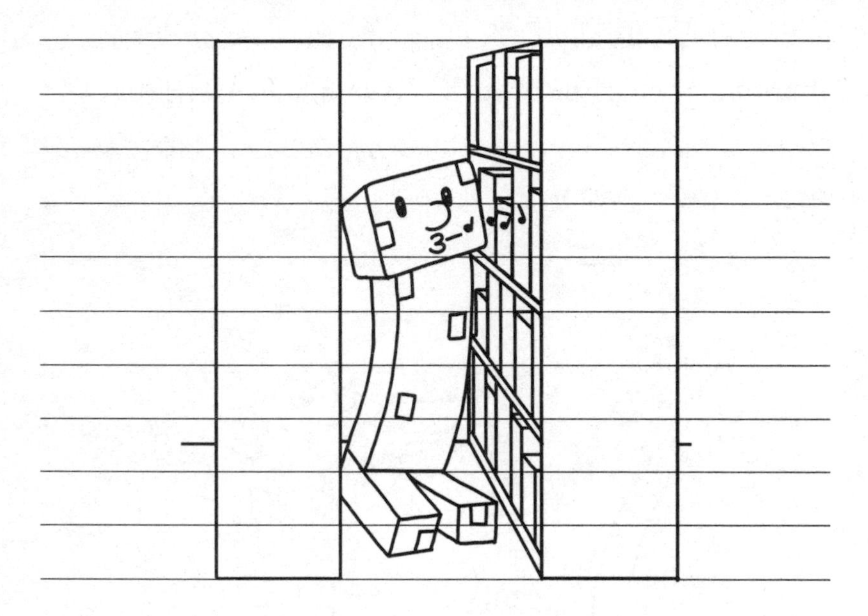

I tell you what, if Mob Middle School ever decides to offer Acting Class, I could TEACH it.

I examined every inch of every book on the first shelf. I turned my head sideways to read the spines. I leaned in and SMELLED those books. I cozied up to them the way Dad does with his tools in the garage, as if they were my own precious babies.

And Mrs. Collins noticed. "Need a book, Gerald?" she asked.

I *pretended* to think about it. Then I shook my head. "Actually, Mrs. Collins, I want to MAKE a book. Ever since you mentioned *those* enchanted books, it's all I can THINK about! I dream about enchanting books someday." Then I sighed super loudly. "I only wish I didn't have to WAIT." I scrunched up my eyes and might have even squirted out a tear.

Well, Mrs. Collins ate my performance right up. She hurried over and patted my back. "There, there, Gerald. I can see how much you LOVE books. And I appreciate your initiative."

As soon as I heard the word "initiative," I knew I was golden. Grown-ups love it when you want to do something BEFORE they ask you to. Like cleaning your room. Or taking out the trash. Or sweeping up the gunpowder after your baby sister's latest explosion.

So by the time Enchantment Class started, Mrs. Collins was practically SHOVING books in my face. While other kids lined up with shears and shovels, I headed to the enchantment table with a book. A few books actually.

I got some weird looks from other kids in class, let me tell you. But I just kept my mouth shut. A creeper never reveals his secrets, right? Besides, if

I let it slip that I had an ANVIL at home, kids would be lining up from clear across the Overworld to get into Dad's garage. And I knew the old man really wouldn't appreciate that.

Mrs. Collins let me enchant two more books while I waited for Sam after school. He gets tutored in the library on Wednesday and Friday mornings—the perfect chance for me to spend extra time in the enchantment room.

By the time I got home this morning, I had FIVE enchanted books. Those glowing purple covers felt like diamonds in my backpack. Sam and I took the LONG way home to make sure that no one followed me and tried to steal them.

Now that I'm back in my room, I've spread them across my bed like treasure loot. Here's what I've got:

- Two books with the Efficiency enchantment. (That one's kind of disappointing. I mean, it'd be great if I were a miner trying to get lots of stuff in one trip to a mineshaft. But I prefer to keep my feet ABOVE ground, thank you very much.)

• One book with Fire Aspect. (That one's for swords, I figured out. Not sure what I'll do with it yet, but I'm thinking I can make a trade . . .)

• One book with Protection. (BINGO! I know EXACTLY what to do with that. I'm going to make some armor to *protect* my green skin from Chloe's flinging fireballs.)

• One book with Respiration. (WOW. I really hit the jackpot there. If I put that enchantment on a helmet, I can actually BREATHE underwater.)

I tried to imagine that. I pressed my face up against Sticky's aquarium and pretended I was floating in there beside him. Sticky had mixed feelings about that, I could tell.

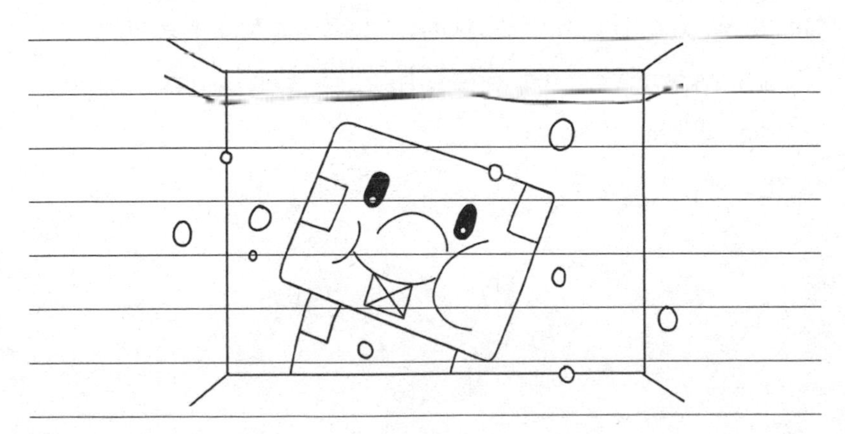

That's right about when Mom burst in and flung open my window.

At first I thought she was going to jump through it, but instead she took this deep breath—as if someone were cooking burnt porkchops outside, and she couldn't get enough of the smell.

Then she said something like, "Now that we've gotten rid of all that clutter, we've cleared the way for POSITIVE energy to flow. Doesn't it feel WONDERFUL, Gerald?"

No, it did not. That positive energy was "flowing" right over my enchanted books. Pages started flapping around. But before she left the room, Mom made me take a deep breath of that fresh air. Three of them, in fact.

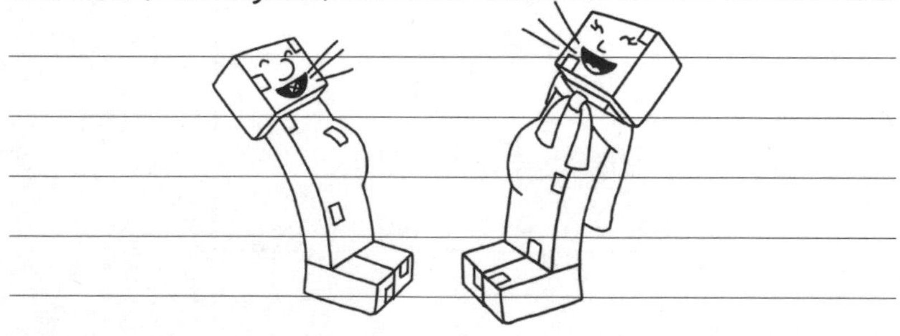

And through that open window, I heard a beautiful sound coming from the garage. *BANG, CLINK, CLANK!*

Dad was back at work on the anvil. Which meant that I'd be enchanting books in no time—by this weekend. Maybe even sooner!

"Right after you finish your homework," Mom reminded me. I swear that creeper is a mind reader.

So now I'm trying to study. Math, History, Enchantments, Science . . . Blah, biddy, blah, blah, blah.

But that's okay. I've got a stack of enchanted books by my bed, and I'll be breathing underwater and swimming like a squid in no time.

DAY 3: SATURDAY

I'm starting to think I'll need to use that Efficiency enchantment on DAD. Because the weekend is here. Dad's been working on the anvil for a whole day, and he's not even close to being finished. At least he SAYS he's not.

When I got home from school this morning, I went straight to the garage. Dad was polishing the anvil with a cloth, humming while he worked. But when I asked if he was almost done, he shook his head. "Not even close," he said. "Nope—lots of work to do on this one, son." He started tinkering with something on the side of the anvil.

Well, Gerald Creeper Sr. can't fool me. I know he's dogging on this project so he can stay in the garage longer—all weekend maybe. But this creep doesn't have that kind of time.

So I'm going to be on him like a wart on a witch's nose. We're getting this thing done tonight—me and Dad.

I told him I'd be back. I gave him that look that says, "I've got my eyes on you, mister." That was when a fireball shot through the open garage window and pinged off my forehead.

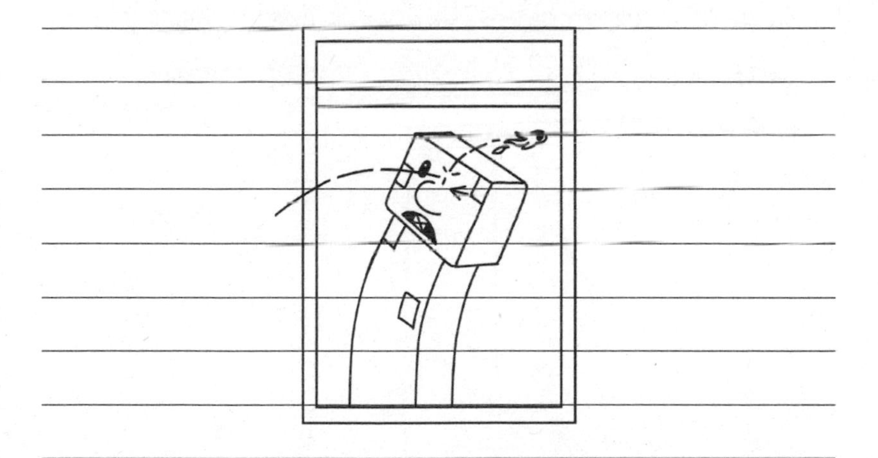

Now that Mom's got windows open everywhere, there's no hiding from Chloe's crummy dispenser. I needed protection—and I needed it FAST. So I dodged another fireball, dove inside the front door, and headed straight to Cate's closet to look for some armor.

At first, Cate was all like, "Don't you ever KNOCK, Gerald?" and "Can't a girl have a little PRIVACY?!" But when she found out what I was looking for, she sprang into action.

Pretty soon, Cate had all kinds of things for me to try on:

- A leather vest that COULD work like a chest plate (after I cut off all the embarrassing fringe from the bottom)

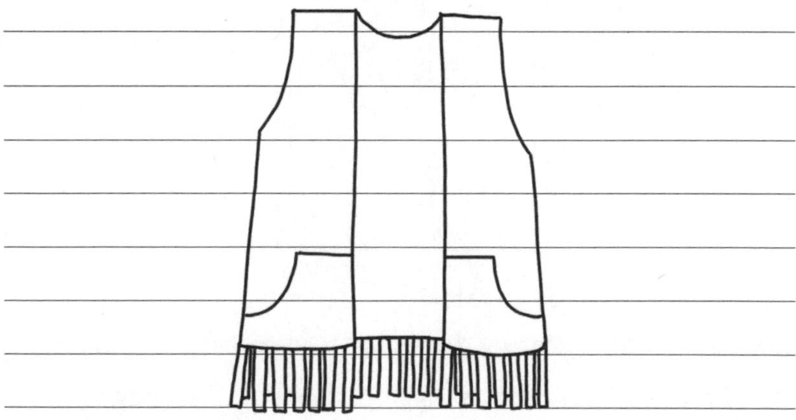

- Clunky leather boots (from Cate's combat fashion phase)

- Leather leggings—that I won't be caught dead in. EVER.

Cate said they were like skinny jeans and super comfy. So I DID try them on—just once. But as soon as I looked in the mirror, I knew. Creepers like me should NOT wear skinny jeans. Or leather leggings. Or any pants out of his sister's closet ever again.

It didn't help when a fireball spat through Cate's window and bounced off my butt. I mean, the leather DID kind of protect me. But I could hear Chloe laughing from clear across the backyard at me in my leggings.

So I peeled them right off, which was NOT easy. (It was like wrestling with a cave spider, or at least trying to get out of its web—which I've done before, by the way. But that's a whole other story.)

Anyway, the one thing Cate didn't have in her closet was a helmet. Not a leather one. Not an iron one. Not ANY kind of one.

So I guess I won't be breathing underwater like Sticky anytime soon. But I CAN enchant some armor to put an end to the fireball attacks. I mean, just as soon as Dad is done with that anvil.

DAY 4: SUNDAY

We did it! WOOT-WOOT!

Last night, Dad and me finished the anvil. (Well, he polished it up some more, tapped it a few times with a pickaxe, and finally declared it DONE.) Then we enchanted my leather vest with Protection.

It worked slick as swamp water. We put my enchanted book into a slot on the anvil, and my new leather vest into the other slot. I heard this clinking sound, like metal on metal. And then? My vest started to glow.

I put that thing on right away, because the garage window was still open, and I KNEW Chloe was watching us with her good buddy Spence the Dispenser. (I'm starting to think that dispenser is evil, that it spits fireballs at me all on its own now—even when Chloe is NOWHERE nearby.)

Anyway, I decided not to cut the fringe off the bottom of the vest, because I need all the protection I can get against Chloe and Spence. And guess what? The Protection enchantment WORKED!

I heard the click of the dispenser, and saw the puff of smoke. But when that flaming spitball hit me, I didn't feel a thing. It might have even TICKLED.

I smiled. Then I started laughing, which made Chloe hissing mad. She launched another gazillion shots at me.

Between you and me, I kind of wish the vest had sleeves. And a hood. And was a bit longer. Because even with the vest on, I took a couple of hits to my legs—and one to my nose.

But I sure wasn't going to let Chloe know that. I just grinned at her and did my annoying "You can't touch this!" dance. That one always gets to her.

I heard Chloe explode, and gunpowder blew through that open window. YES! Chalk one up for Gerald Creeper Jr.

So maybe Mom was right. The positive energy IS flowing, and it sure feels good. I even took a good long whiff. I didn't smell burnt porkchops, but I smelled the next best thing:

SUCCESS.

DAY 6: TUESDAY

Wow, the positive energy is flowing alright! Last night, I came up with the BEST idea ever for a science project. And I actually have BONES to thank for it.

But let me start at the beginning.

We were sitting in Enchantment Class waiting to enchant our fishing rods. I was hoping for Luck of the Sea, but every other mob in class was hoping for Lure. See, the Lure enchantment helps you catch more fish. But Luck of the Sea helps you catch enchanted BOOKS. And who'd want to catch a bunch of floppy fish when they could be loading up on enchantments?

Of course, I ended up getting Lure. (SIGH.) So I pulled my fishing rod right out of the enchantment table and enchanted a book instead.

Bones actually snorted when I did that. "Aw, look at little creepy-weepy, who wants to bring home another bedtime story." He stuck his bony thumb in his mouth and started slurping on it.

I wanted to act like a baby right then—like my baby sister, CAMMY, anyway. She would have blown sky-high and wiped that sneer right off of Bones's skull.

But I reminded myself that Bones just didn't get it. NONE of the mobs in Enchantment Class cared about enchanting books yet. Why? Because none of them had a secret ANVIL at home. And that's just how I wanted to keep it. When it comes to winning the science fair, I—Gerald Creeper Jr.—will take every advantage I can get.

When Sam stuck his fishing rod in the enchantment table, he got Lure, too. He started jiggling with joy, thinking about all the fish he could catch for Moo.

But Willow ended up with MY enchantment—Luck of the Sea. And she was actually DISAPPOINTED. I guess she wanted Lure so she could catch pufferfish to brew more potion of water breathing.

Again with the potions? I was kind of done with that topic. So I asked Willow why she didn't just wait till next week, when we would learn how to enchant armor. I said maybe she could enchant a helmet with Respiration, and breathe underwater that way. I mean, we were in ENCHANTMENT class, for crying out loud—not POTIONS class.

But Willow is all about her potions. She just shrugged. "Potions are better than enchantments," she said, like she was stating some fact out of a science book.

Then Bones started whining again about enchanting his bow. And Mrs. Collins said NO, we were still enchanting tools this week. So Bones reached into his backpack and pulled out the only "tools" I've ever seen him use: a pair of drumsticks.

I hate to admit it, but Bones is a wicked good drummer. Now I didn't know that you could enchant drumsticks. I don't think Mrs. Collins knew it either. When he stuck those drumsticks in the enchantment table, her mouth dropped right open.

But sure enough, the sticks started glowing purple. I guess Bones got the Efficiency enchantment—the one miners use. And when he drummed them on the table, those sticks FLEW.

He had this crazy beat going. Everyone stopped to listen, and a couple of teachers stuck their heads in the doorway.

Finally Mrs. Collins cleared her throat and told Bones he should probably "take those sticks home and use them there."

Well, I was already dreaming about ways that I could use the Efficiency enchantment, too. Could I enchant my own MOUTH, so I could be an amazing rapper, like my idol Kid Z? Nah. I wasn't crazy about the idea of sticking my face in the enchantment table.

Then I *thought* about the rap songs I write for Language Arts, and genius struck like a lightning bolt. (It happens to me sometimes. What can I say?) Could I WRITE raps faster with the Efficiency enchantment?

Well, *there* was only one way to find out. Two ways, in fact. Because I *had* TWO books at *home* enchanted with Efficiency.

As soon as I got home, I headed into the garage armed with an enchanted book and a sharp pencil. And when I got out, I couldn't WAIT to start my homework. That glowing pencil jittered, as if it couldn't wait to meet up with a piece of paper either.

Well, let me tell you, I whipped right through my homework. I barely had time to READ my math problems before the answers flowed out the tip of that pencil.

It felt just like the time I got hyped up on caffeine. I had WAY too much hot chocolate at the Creeper Café, and then stayed up all day to finish a couple of homework assignments.

Yeah, this felt kind of like that. Except my homework didn't take me all day—it took me like two minutes.

I zoomed through my science worksheet so fast, I ripped a hole in the paper. Then I scratched out a rap song in about three seconds flat. I'm not even kidding! I swear I saw a trail of smoke jetting out from behind that pencil.

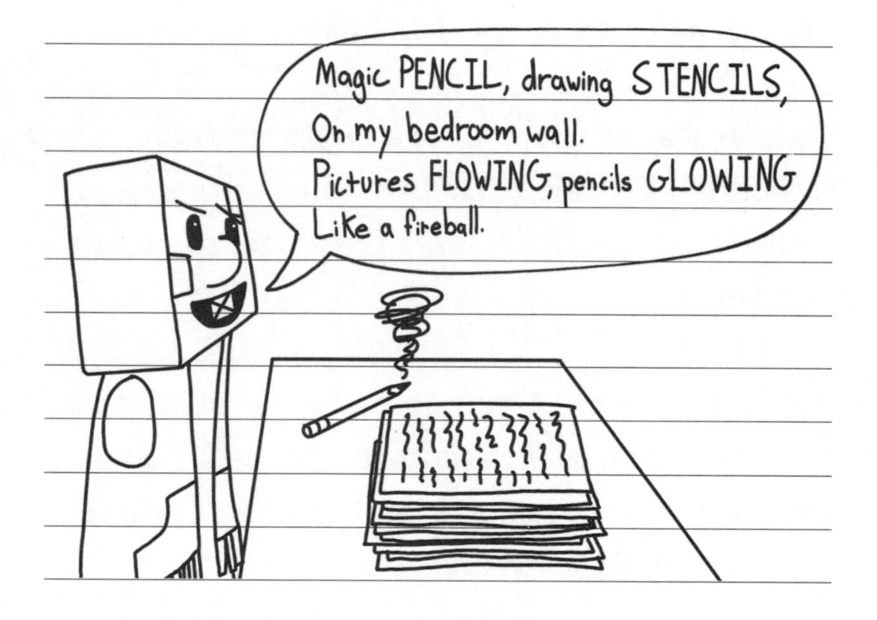

So I'm starting to think this enchanted pencil could be my ticket to fortune and fame—or at least to a stellar science fair project.

Yup, this pencil is my new best friend. (Sorry, Sam.) From this moment on, I'm going to have to keep it with me at ALL times.

DAY 8: THURSDAY

I don't think a creep should have just ONE best friend. So I didn't stop with that enchanted pencil. Nope, I gave myself another little buddy: an enchanted magnifying glass. Why, you ask?

Because now I can not only WRITE fast, but I can READ at the speed of light, too. I know—genius, right?

Suddenly, I'm like the best student at Mob Middle School EVER. I burn through my homework. I write crazy good rap songs—FAST. I'm the first one done with quizzes in class. Yesterday in math, I actually had time to take a NAP after a test.

When my math teacher looked at me funny, I realized that I should probably keep this Efficiency enchantment on the down low. I CAN'T get my enchanted pencil taken away—at least not before

I've figured out how to use it to win the science fair.

But I'm working on ideas. And now that I can get my homework done in record time, I'll have PLENTY of time this weekend to work on the science project, right?

RIGHT!

DAY 10: SATURDAY

By Golem, I've GOT it. A science fair project, that is.

It's only Saturday morning, and I've already made a HUGE poster for the fair. I wrote down lots of numbers—stats on how fast I can do my homework with an enchanted pencil and magnifying glass, and how SLOW I am without them. I drew LOTS of charts and graphs, too. (Teachers and judges eat up that sort of thing.)

So this creep is feeling pretty good about himself, I've got to say. It's only been a week and a half, and I've almost polished off my whole 30-day plan:

30-Day Plan to a Stellar Science Project

- Convince Dad to help me build an anvil. ✓
- Use enchanted books to come up with an AWESOME science project. ✓✓
- Burn Chloe with my project—and take home enough emeralds to buy a jukebox! (Yup, I can hear those rap songs pouring out of the jukebox already.)
- Oh, and avoid Mom (before she donates me and everything I love to charity) (So far, so good. I'm still here, right?)

The way I see it, Mom is the only thing that could get in the way of my plan. Now that the weekend is here, she's doing what she calls her "second wave" of cutting clutter. GREAT.

There's barely anything left in the house as it is! Sock the Sheep is still in the backyard, but Mom took a pair of shears to him—like his wool was extra clutter too. The poor naked sheep is looking through my open window right now, like he wants to crawl in and hide under my bed.

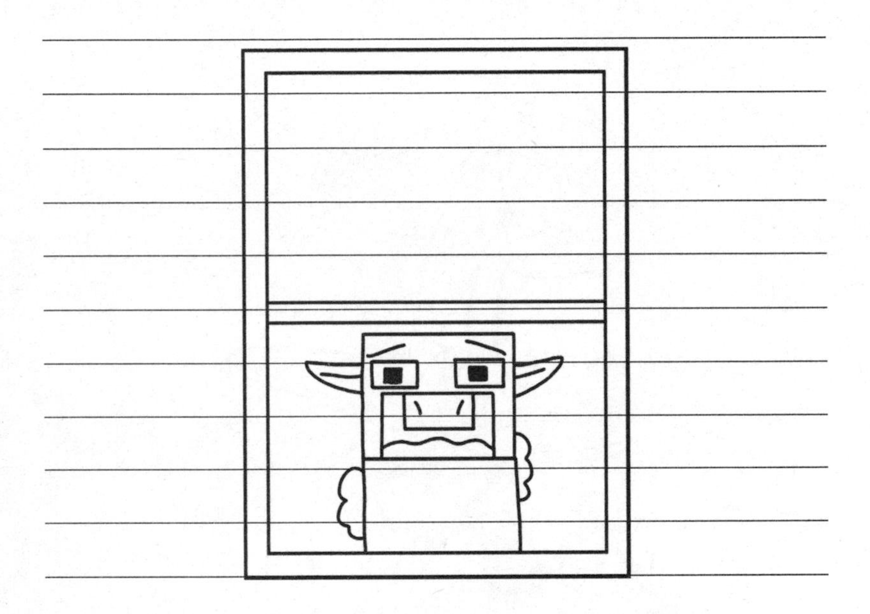

So if Mom's still at it, I'm going to have to hold tight to my enchanted pencil. And to my science fair poster. Because my leather vest can protect me from fireballs and flaming arrows, but it can't protect me from Mom the Clutter Control Queen.

DAY 13: TUESDAY

I will NEVER speak to Sam the Slime again as long as I live. At least not when he's wearing a dumb leather helmet on his ginormous green head.

He actually came to school wearing it. I mean, sure, it's finally "armor and weapons" week in Enchantment Class. But that class isn't until after lunch. Was Sam going to wear that helmet ALL DAY? And how did he squeeze his head into the thing in the first place? It looked like his head might pop, and his brains might gush right out.

I said so while we were standing by our lockers in between classes. But Sam couldn't hear me—not with his ears all squished up in that helmet.

He didn't hear me later, either, when I told him about my science project. I had to tell SOMEONE, for crying out loud. The secret was bubbling up inside me like hot mushroom stew.

But I had to repeat it twice. I told Sam to take the helmet off so he could hear me, but I guess it was stuck or something. So I told him about my science project ONE MORE TIME—loudly.

And Mrs. Collins just happened to be walking by at that exact second. GREAT.

She lowered her reading glasses, stared at me hard, and pulled me into the library. I HOPED she was going to compliment me on my enchanted leather vest with the fringe on the bottom. But she didn't.

Instead, she proceeded to tell me that I could NOT use enchantments to get my homework done faster. That would be CHEATING, she said. And other teachers might get upset. And we might have to cancel Enchantment Class. "And that wouldn't be fair to other students now, would it, Gerald?" she asked.

Not fair to OTHER students? What about ME? I wanted to say. I mean, Bones got away with enchanting his drumsticks, didn't he?

But Mrs. Collins wasn't hearing it. She asked me to hand over my enchanted pencil AND my enchanted magnifying glass. RIGHT NOW.

Maybe if I'd had more time to think, I could have faked some tears or come up with a perfectly good reason why I needed to keep my things. But I couldn't. My brain was on lock-down, and when I tried to squeeze out a tear, my insides started hissing and bubbling. I was going to blow sky-high—I could feel it. And teachers don't really appreciate that sort of thing.

So instead, I crept off down the hall. I might as well have crept right out the front door and all the way home. Because it's all over for me now. I should just hand Chloe her emeralds for best science fair project. And lean over and let her zing me with a batch of fireballs, while I'm at it.

Click. Puff. Zing.

Stick a fork in me, because this creeper is DONE.

DAY 15: THURSDAY

You know what's super annoying about Sam? It's REALLY hard to stay mad at that slime. Especially when he's all wrapped up in tinsel like a Christmas tree.

Well, it wasn't really tinsel. It was supposed to be a chain chestplate. But Sam is as wide as he is tall, and round as a ball. So it takes a LOT of chain to wrap that boy up.

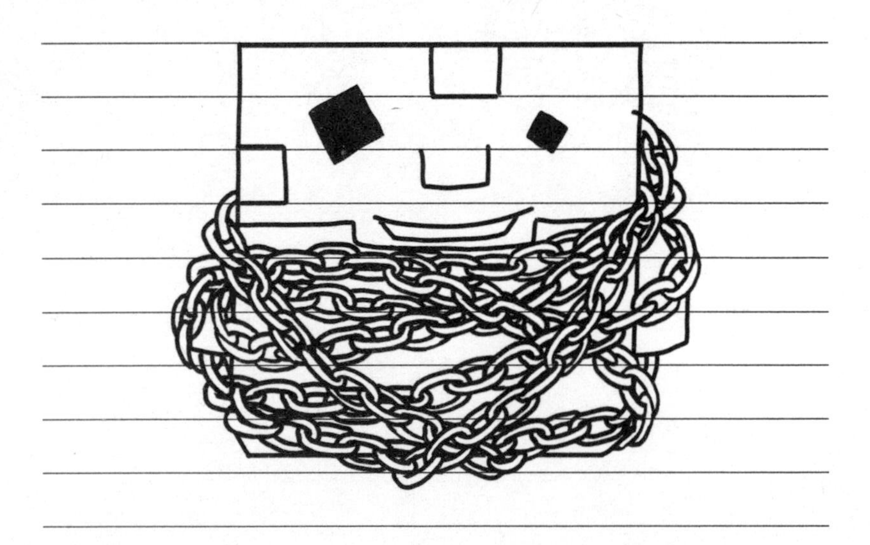

See, I guess the leather helmet wasn't really working out for Sam—it gave him a headache. (Go figure.) So now he's all blinged out in silver, like Kid Z in his chains. But WAY less cool.

Anyway, it was hard to look at Sam without laughing. And I REALLY didn't want him to see me smiling just yet—I was still pretty mad about the whole "turn in your enchanted pencil" incident. I'd had a perfectly good science project. And now, thanks to Sam and his too-tight helmet? I had nothing. Zilch. Zero. Nada.

PLUS, it took me TWO HOURS to get my homework done this morning. I forgot how boring it was to do it the old-fashioned way, with a slow, dull pencil.

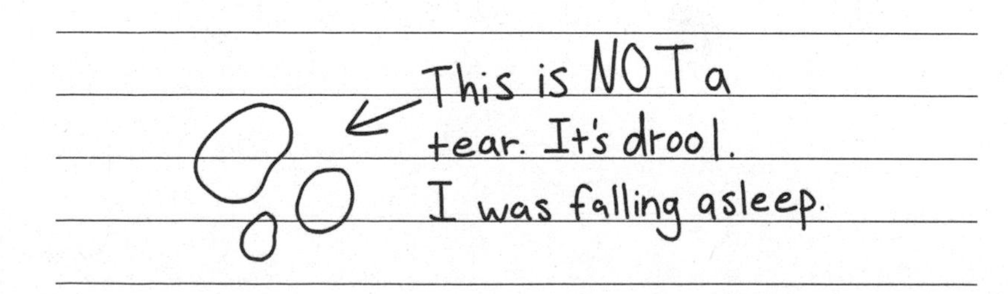

Even my rap song for Language Arts turned out to be a total embarrassment.

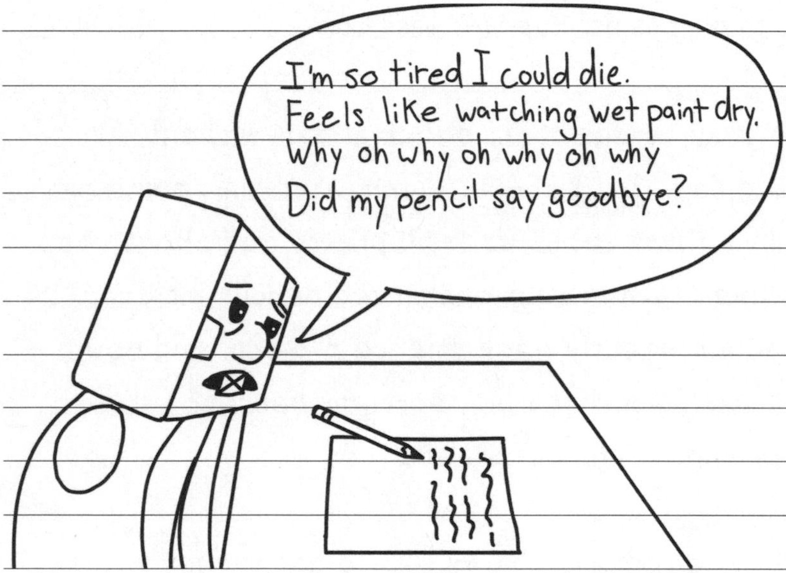

I'm so tired I could die.
Feels like watching wet paint dry.
Why oh why oh why oh why
Did my pencil say goodbye?

This IS a tear stain.
I really, REALLY miss my enchanted pencil (sniff).

So yeah, I was still steaming mad at Sam. But I forgot all about that when I saw what Willow Witch brought to class. A SWORD. YIKES.

She was standing at the enchantment table, complaining about getting the Fire Aspect enchantment instead of the Bane of Arthropods.

I guess that Arthropods one would make it easier for her to "collect" spider eyes for potions. BLECH.

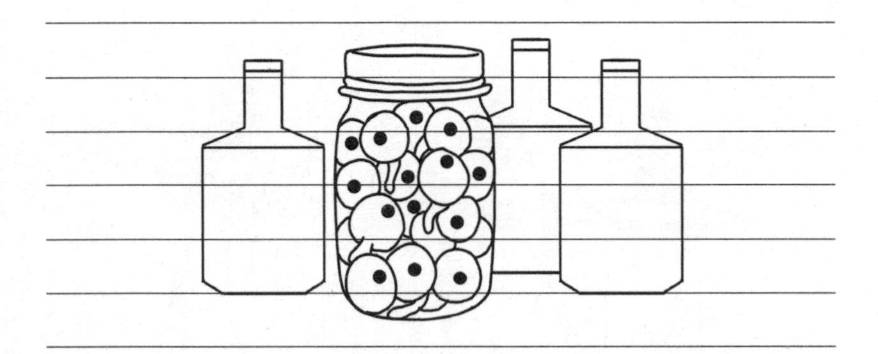

Bones was in line behind the witches, and he was PUMPED UP. Now that it's weapons week, he's been enchanting all his bows to make them more powerful. GREAT. He rubbed his bony hands together the way Dad does when we make fireworks in the garage.

Which enchantment would Bones get? POWER, to make his arrows more damaging? FLAME, so he could set things on fire with them? INFINITY, so he could shoot as many arrows as he wanted and NEVER use them up?

WHO CARES??? They're ALL unfair, if you ask me. Why can a bully like Bones run around with flaming arrows, when a harmless creep like me can't even keep an enchanted PENCIL?

SHEESH.

When Bones got the Infinity enchantment, Mrs. Collins reminded him that he could ONLY use his enchanted bows during extracurricular activities. But I happen to know that one of his "extracurriculars" is picking on mobs like me. So I made sure my leather vest was good and snug around my shoulders.

When Sam got his turn at the enchantment table, he ended up with the Protection enchantment. He was SO excited. He started bragging about how he could roll through lava without getting burned. How he could bounce right off cactus plants. (He even demonstrated that with the cactus in the corner, which I'll admit was KIND of cool. Me and cactus plants don't exactly get along.)

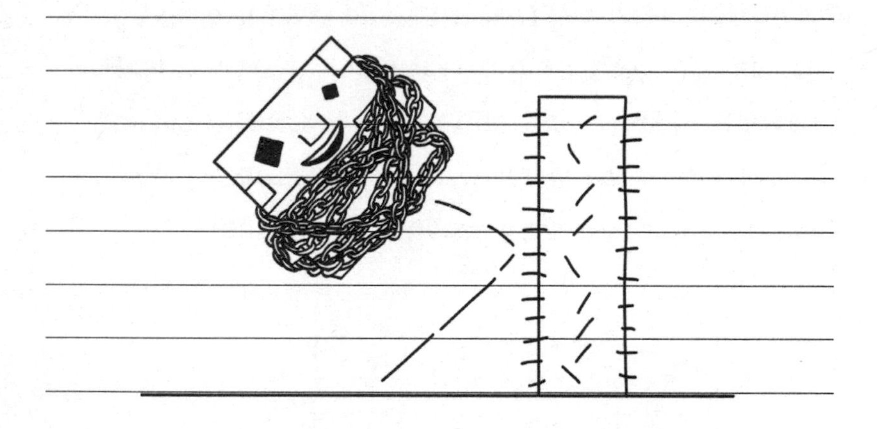

But now Bones was staring at Sam, like he was a shiny new target or something. I could tell his fingers were itchy to try out his enchanted bow. So I was going to have to walk Sam home after school, no matter how mad I was at him. Someone had to have that slime's bouncy back.

When it was MY turn to enchant something, I wasn't even excited. Sure, I had Cate's boots. And I ended up getting the Depth Strider enchantment, which would help me swim faster. But so what? I'd already given up on the whole "breathe underwater" thing, since I couldn't find a single helmet in Cate's closet.

Funny, how I needed a helmet and didn't have one. And how Sam had one, but couldn't wear it. And . . . well, you can see where I'm going with this. Genius struck again while I was standing right there at the enchantment table.

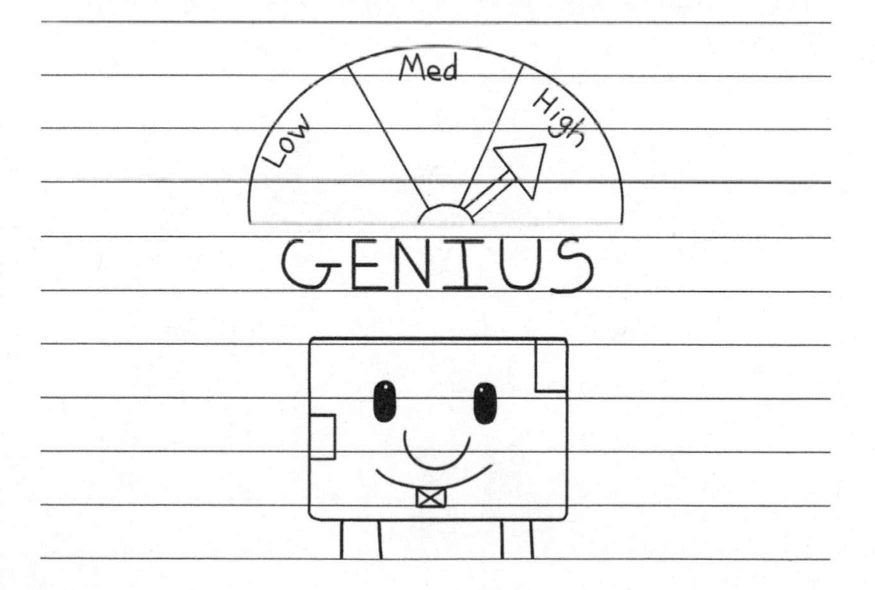

Now I FOR SURE had to walk Sam home. As soon as we left school, I came straight out and asked him if I could have his helmet. (Well, I might have said "borrow.") But Sam barely heard me. He was bouncing off every tree and rock, testing out his enchanted chest plate.

Then it happened. An ARROW bounced off Sam's back.

I whirled around and spotted Bones on the edge of the Archery field. He dropped his bow, looked up at the sky, and started whistling. But his gang of rattler friends were laughing their bony butts off.

Well, Sam didn't even know what hit him. He just kept on bouncing around and grinning. So I gotta say, that Protection enchantment REALLY works. But it does NOT mean that Bones and his buddies can use Sam for target practice.

I'm proud to say that I actually stepped in front of Sam—at least until the next arrow hit. Because that one was FLAMING. Yup, Sam would have been one smoked slime, if not for his enchanted armor.

That's when I decided it would be better for me to use HIM as MY shield. I mean, Sam doesn't have to worry about taking a flaming arrow to the leg like I do. And if I get hit, who's going to walk Sam home?

Well, those arrows kept coming. Of COURSE they did, because Bones was trying out his new Infinity enchantment. I almost wished Willow would show up with her enchanted sword, because she is one FIERCE witch when someone messes with her boy, Sam.

But she didn't.

When we finally made it back to Sam's house alive, I asked him about his helmet. I told him it was probably my next best chance at a science project, and that he kind of owed it to me, after the whole "Mrs. Collins took my pencil" thing.

Well, when Sam said YES, I did my happy dance. He ran right into the house and bounced out with that leather helmet. It was a LITTLE bit stretched out from his big noggin, but I figured it would still work. Then he asked if I wanted to go fishing this weekend.

Um, let me think about that, I told him. See, I'm not really big on fishing. (I had a pretty traumatic experience fishing with my dad in the jungle last summer, but THAT's a whole other story.)

Sam kept pleading. And then I got to thinking that if I had my enchanted helmet and boots, maybe I could SWIM in the lake while he fished. And figure out a NEW stellar science project.

Anyway, like I said, I didn't commit to Sam right away. I learned a long time ago that a creeper has to keep his options open.

DAY 17: SATURDAY

So, I went fishing with Sam tonight. Turns out, it was my best option.

I mean, I could have stayed home and done homework. But I was sick and tired of staring at the pile of books on my desk. It's been growing taller by the minute, I swear. I think I even heard it growl at me, trying to get my attention.

But I am NOT doing homework on a Saturday. I don't even feel like writing raps anymore. (Did I really just SAY that?!)

I guess I could have stayed home and let Chloe pelt me with chicken eggs. (Yup, you heard me right.) When I went out to the garage to enchant my helmet with Respiration, I heard the CLICK of Spence the Dispenser. I saw the puff of smoke. And I did NOTHING. Because, I mean, I'm wearing my enchanted vest, right?

But it turns out, Chloe has moved on from fireballs and started using CHICKEN EGGS. (I guess there were some left over after Mom gave the chickens away.)

Well, my enchanted vest DOES protect against chicken eggs. They bounce right off. But most of Chloe's rotten eggs hit me in the FACE. Or bounced off my vest and cracked open on my legs and feet. And Chloe thinks it's all one big yolk—er, JOKE.

So, no thank you. I was not going to stay home on a Saturday night with my egg-flinging Evil Twin.

The other reason I decided to go fishing is because Thanksgiving is only FIVE days away. That means Aunt

Constance is coming, and Mom is totally freaking out. She tore through the house AGAIN, cleaning and looking for ANYTHING else she could get rid of. When she started getting rid of furniture, I knew we were in trouble.

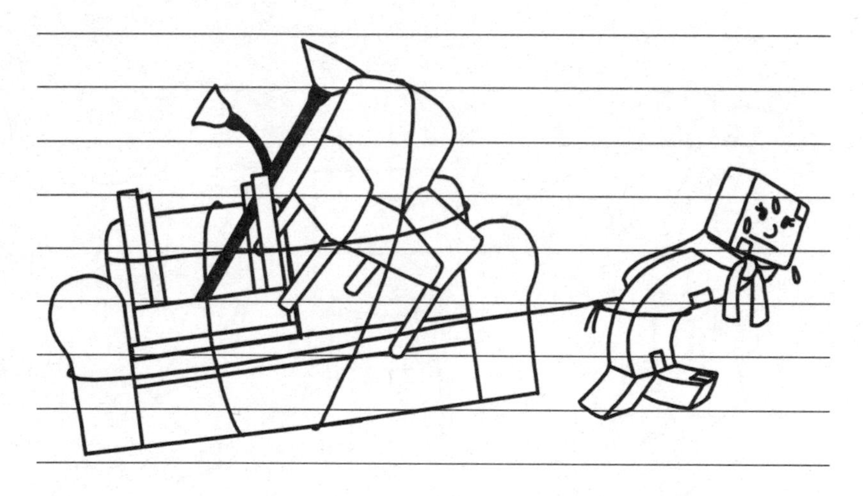

There's a big empty spot in the living room where the rocking chair used to be. And you know what Mom stuck in its place? A CACTUS plant. Creepers don't even LIKE ~~cactuses~~ ~~CACTI~~ those kinds of plants!

But Mom started talking about positive energy again, and about reconnecting with our "Life Force"

(HUH?), and about how we need more WIND and WATER and GREENERY in the house.

More wind? The windows are pretty much open ALL the time now. If griefers wanted to come in and steal our stuff, Mom's making it REALLY easy for them—I mean, except for the fact that we don't have any stuff left to steal.

And as for greenery? There are six creepers living in this house, so I think we're pretty green already. Just saying . . .

When Mom mentioned water, I breathed a sigh of relief—I'm not gonna lie. Because that means Sticky is probably safe in his aquarium. My pet squid won't end up in a donation box, headed to poor mobs in the Nether, anytime soon.

I probably shouldn't have even THOUGHT about Sticky, because Mind-Reader Mom handed me a rag and said she wanted me to clean Sticky's aquarium till it sparkled.

But I thought fast. I told Mom that even though I really, REALLY wanted to clean the aquarium, I was feeling the need for more WATER in my life. In fact, Sam and I were heading to the lake tonight, where we could breathe in all that positive energy and reconnect with our life force—blah, biddy, blah, blah, blah.

And Mom ate it right up. Or maybe she just didn't hear me, because she was sliding a row of pictures off the wall and putting them in a cardboard box.

So that's how I ended up fishing with Sam. By the time I got to the lake with my enchanted helmet and boots, I was imagining my new science project. I could picture the poster already.

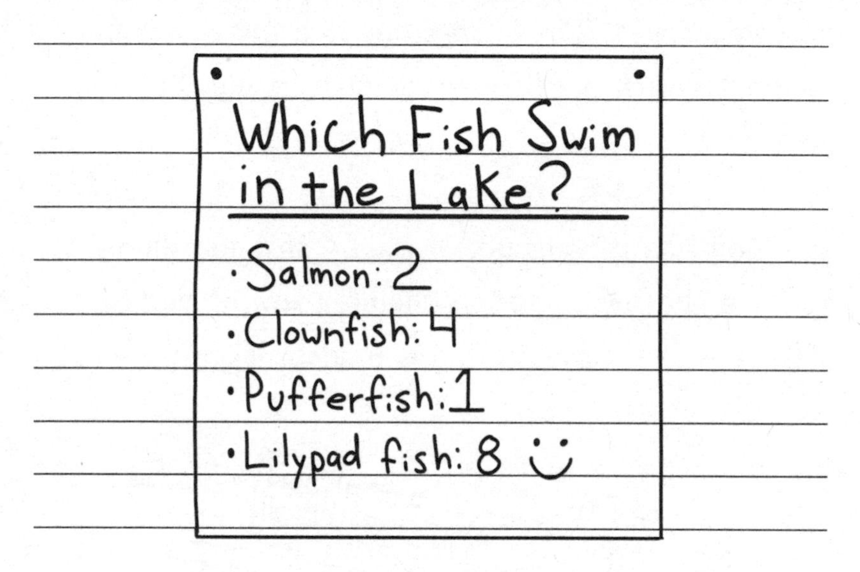

But that poster went up in smoke when Sam showed up at the lake with Moo.

SERIOUSLY?!

That cat KNOWS I'm not a fan of hers. And she really likes to rub it in. How? By rubbing ALL OVER my legs. Good thing I had my Depth Strider boots on during that "love fest." I could barely WAIT to get into the water and away from Moo.

But Sam wanted me to fish with him. Every time I put on my helmet and started wading into the lake, he was all like, "Gerald, I think I got something!" He'd yank his pole out of the water, and then he'd show me the big lily pad hanging off the hook. I wasn't sure Sam's Lure enchantment was actually working. Even Moo was drooling, waiting and wondering when that fishing rod was going to catch a fish.

I was almost relieved when Willow showed up with her fishing rod, too. Maybe she could keep Sam busy ABOVE water while I was doing my science project IN the water. I barely said hello to her before I pulled on my helmet, took a deep breath, and dove in.

Well, the first thing that happened was that water GUSHED into Sam's stretched-out helmet. I started to panic, but then I remembered that I could BREATHE underwater wearing that enchanted helmet. It was like being in a dream—the one I've had for eons about swimming with Sticky in his aquarium. And with my Depth Strider boots, I could swim FAST. I raced against a clownfish, and actually won! Boy, was that fish surprised.

So, yeah, breathing underwater was pretty cool. For about 15 seconds. That's how long the enchanted helmet lasts before you start choking and spitting up water. And that part's NOT cool.

Willow had to pat me on the back. I think I actually burped up a tiny fish, which Moo was all over. Then she rubbed up against me again, and before I knew it, I was COVERED in sticky wet cat hair.

GROSS.

Sam was all like, "Wow! I didn't know Moo even LIKED water!"

"She DOESN'T," I groaned. "Cats hate water. Every mob knows that." And now I kind of hated water too. There's nothing like a near-drowning experience to make you rethink your science project—and pretty much your whole life.

"Moo only likes my BOOTS," I told Sam. "Probably because they smell like clownfish."

That's when a torch must have lit up inside his head, because he bounced up and announced that he had an idea for his science fair project.

Say WHAT now?

"Armor for cats. Get it?" said Sam. "Instead of enchanted, I said, en-CAT-ed!" Then he fell all over himself laughing.

Yeah, I got the joke. But it was pretty much the WORST idea I'd heard in my whole entire life.

Sam had it all planned out. He'd sew little leather booties for Moo and try to enchant them with Depth Strider. He'd make her a little leather bonnet and enchant it with Respiration. "You can wear it on your little headie-weddie," he cooed to Moo.

That was when I lost it. "That's NOT science," I said to Sam.

"Sure it is!" he said. "I'm going to do an experiment to see if I can get a cat to like water. MY cat anyway."

Well, I wanted to argue. But Willow suddenly got a bite on her fishing line. When she pulled an enchanted BOOK out of the water, we all sprang to attention. Even Moo sniffed and licked at the dripping-wet book.

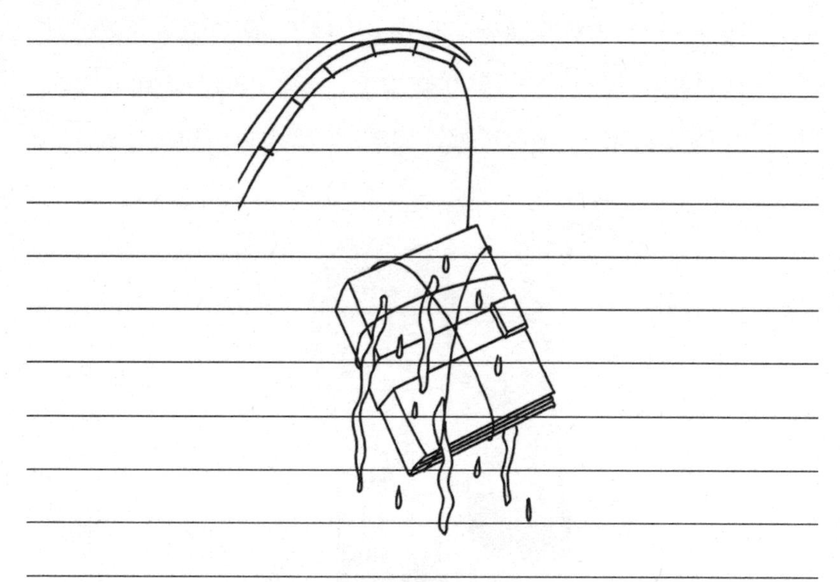

"Frost Walker!" Willow announced.

WOW. She'd gotten one of those enchantments you can ONLY get from treasure chests, trades, or fishing. Frost Walker would let Willow walk ON the water, instead of trying to swim in it. It would actually turn the water to ICE.

Well, I couldn't believe her luck—until I remembered she was fishing with the Luck of the Sea enchantment.

You'd think a witch would be pretty excited about Frost Walker, right? I mean, what mob WOULDN'T want to walk on water?

But she turned to Sam and said, "Maybe you can use this enchantment to help MOO learn to like water."

SHEESH. What a colossal WASTE of an enchantment.

When Sam got all weepy and lovey-dovey with Willow, I knew I had to shut things down. "But how is Sam going to USE that enchanted book?" I asked. "Mrs. Collins won't let us use the anvil at school yet!"

Willow narrowed her eyes. "Maybe he can use YOUR anvil," she said.

Say WHAT???

I almost asked her how she knew, but why bother? Witches have all kinds of ways of finding things out. For all I knew, she'd been spying on me with her potion of invisibility.

So instead, I thought fast. "My anvil is . . . um . . . damaged," I said. "Chloe got a little carried away with her fireball dispenser."

But Willow just shrugged. "Mrs. Collins says we can start using the anvil at school next week," she said.

HUH. So much for my "secret weapon" at home. If all the kids started using enchanted books and anvils, I'd NEVER come up with the award-winning science fair project. There'd be way too much competition.

Like Moo and his en-CAT-ed armor.

GREAT. I suddenly felt like I'd dived into the lake and hit rock bottom. Things were looking up for Sam and his science project. And for Moo, who'd get to walk on water any day now. And for Willow, who could care less about enchantments, but kept getting cool ones anyway.

But for me? Things were looking *pretty* bleak. I'd just about drowned in *that* lake, which meant I probably needed to come up with a new science project. And I was drowning in *homework*, too.

While I dumped the water out of my boots and wrung out my leather helmet, I must have been whining about my life—out loud. Because Willow told me to stop being so dramatic. Then she cracked some joke about needing an enchantment to protect against drama.

BAH-HA-HA. Very funny.

What I really needed was an enchantment to protect me from lousy friends. And sticky wet cat hair.

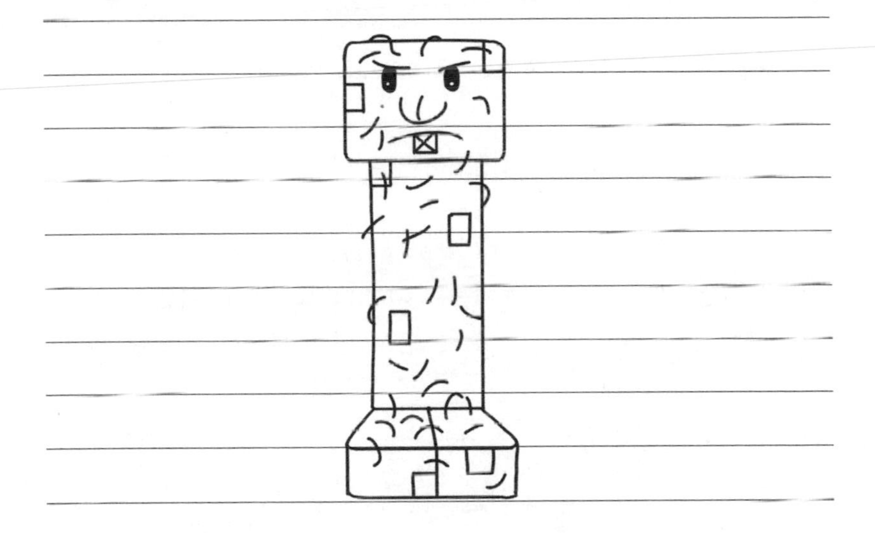

I'm back home now, and I'm still coughing up water—and hairballs. But what's NOT coming up? New ideas for a science project. The fair is only two weeks away, and I have to start all over.

AGAIN.

I flung my window open wider and stood there, hoping for a blast of Mom's positive energy. When I heard something whiz toward me, I thought it might be my Life Force. I raised my face toward the starry sky and took a deep breath.

But NOPE. It wasn't my Life Force at all.

It was just a chicken egg.

SPLAT.

DAY 18: SUNDAY

You know, I like to think I'm a *pretty* RE-SIL-I-ENT creeper. That means when Life gets me down, I find a way to bounce back up—like a slime. Usually.

Tonight was kind of like *that*.

I was going to stay in and feel sorry for myself. When Sam came over and invited me to go fishing with him and Willow again, I almost said no. Why would I want to hang out with a wet cat and a witch who kept pulling out enchanted books from the lake—and didn't even APPRECIATE them?

But then I saw Mom carrying another cactus plant into the house. And I really didn't appreciate THAT either. So I grabbed my fishing rod and got out of there—FAST. I didn't even bring my boots and helmet this time. I mean, a creeper has to cut his losses.

Well, I'm sure glad I went fishing with Sam tonight. Because you know what happened? He gave me a genius new idea for a science project. Well, actually, WILLOW gave me the idea.

Here's how it all went down:

Sam had caught like his tenth lily pad, and then finally caught a fish. A SALMON.

He was about to feed that raw fish to Moo, which would have been a total waste. But then Willow pulled her enchanted SWORD from out of nowhere. (You never know what a witch might be hiding in her purple robe.) She touched the tip of it to that fish and lit it on fire.

I'd forgotten all about the Fire Aspect enchantment she'd put on that sword! But my eyes—and nose—were all over that burning fish. When the flames went out, it was black and crispy, just the way I like it. When Sam cut it into four equal pieces, I nearly swallowed mine whole.

He caught another salmon right away. I guess his Lure enchantment was finally kicking in. And after a few more burned, crispy bites of salmon, my brain started to kick in, too. Nothing like a good meal to set things right again.

So here's what I started thinking:

Maybe I could use the Fire Aspect enchantment with something OTHER than a sword. Like an experiment—a SCIENCE experiment. I mean, Fire Aspect would come in really handy for, say, a knife. Or a spatula. Or a FORK.

YES! I could see it already: a fork that burned ANY food to a crisp. I could make crispy little potatoes in a flash. I'd whip up Mom's apple crisp for dessert, just by plunging my Flaming Fork into an apple! And I could have burnt porkchops—my favorite food—for EVERY meal of every day.

When my stomach growled, I knew I was on to something. Sure, the enchanted pencil had been cool. And breathing underwater might be pretty fun for SOME creep. But the Flaming Fork? This was my best idea YET.

As soon as I got home this morning, I dug through the kitchen drawers looking for the perfect tool. But Mom had pretty much cleaned those drawers right out. There were like seven forks lined up in a row—one for each of us, and I guess one for Aunt Constance. Seven spoons. Seven knives.

I COULDN'T take one of those. Mom would be on to me in a flash.

So I went to the only part of the house that still had STUFF—Dad's garage. I think he's been napping out there lately, since Mom got rid of the couch in the living room and replaced it with a few pillows and cactus plants.

While Dad snored from a cot in the corner, I searched through his rusty bins and buckets. And I found the PERFECT tool. It's this big fork with a long handle, like something you could use to roast hot dogs on a campfire.

And since I was out in the garage, I decided to do a little enchanting too. Fork in one side of the anvil, book in the other, and VOILA! The Flaming Fork was born. And it works!

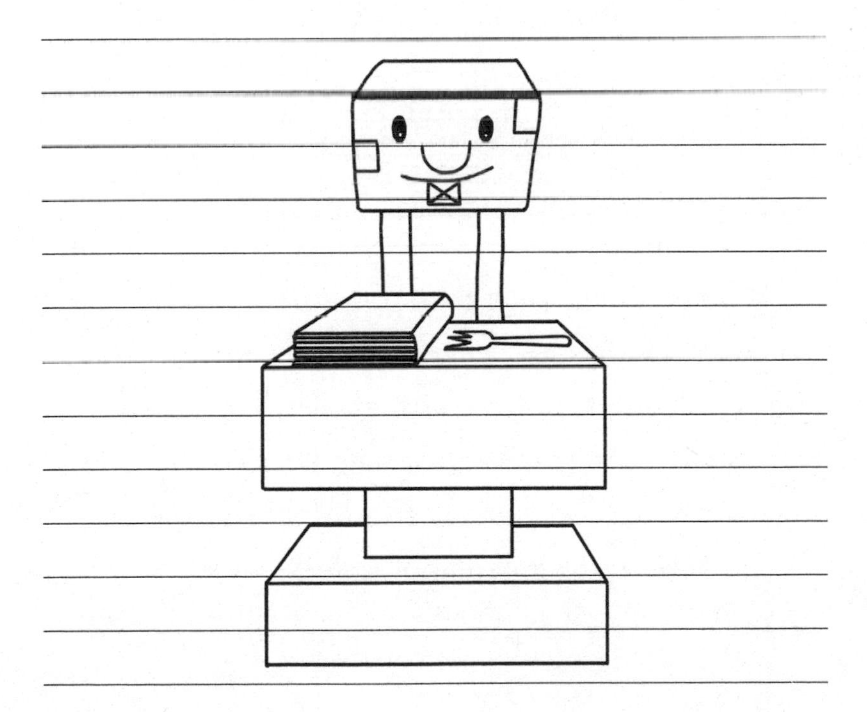

How do I know? Because *that* was an *hour* ago, and I'm already STUFFED with burnt, crispy things. (Burp.)

Everything I *touch* with *that* fork *turns* into flaming deliciousness. In fact, when I was coming out of *the* garage, Chloe *pelted* me with a chicken egg. And guess what? I *touched* my Flaming Fork *to the* egg running off my boot, and it fried right *up*. I ate it off *the* fork, right in front of Chloe's eyes. HA!!!

She turned three shades of green and blew sky high. Which means that my NEW science project is WAY better than hers.

Yup, my 30-day plan is back on track. Maybe instead of staying OUT of Mom's way, I'll even give the gal a hand in the kitchen on Thanksgiving. Because THAT's the kind of son I am.

DAY 21: WEDNESDAY

So it's official: my Flaming Fork improves the taste of EVERYTHING.

I was sitting at lunch last night, and all I could smell was the stench from Ziggy Zombie's rotten-flesh sandwich. So when he wasn't looking, I pulled my Flaming Fork out of my backpack. As I touched the soggy flesh hanging from the side of that sandwich, I tried not to hurl.

When flames shot up from his sandwich, Ziggy sure looked surprised. And he wasn't all that happy about his meat being cooked. (I think zombies prefer things raw and runny.) But I'll tell you what: my fork sure took care of that smell!

I even used my Flaming Fork to improve the hot lunch they were serving in the cafeteria. "Meatloaf," the menu on the wall read. But between you and me, I'm pretty sure Ms. Wilma, the cafeteria lady, sneaks a little rotten flesh into her meatloaf.

So when she was serving some kid a sloppy pile of mashed potatoes, I snuck over to the warming plate in the cafeteria line. And I gave a few of those meatloaf slices a makeover with my Flaming Fork.

Well, the mobs in line behind me RAVED about that meal. All of a sudden, bag lunches started getting thrown in the trash, and kids lined up for rotten-flesh meatloaf.

So I'm for sure going to help Mom make her Thanksgiving meal tomorrow. She and Aunt Constance will be BLOWN AWAY by my cooking skills. Maybe they'll help me sell my Flaming Fork to restaurants across the Overworld. Maybe I'll be awarded Top Chef on a cooking show. Maybe I'll have my OWN show someday!

Yeah, the science fair is just the start. This Flaming Fork is going to earn me a jukebox for sure—and a one-way ticket to Fame and Fortune. I can hardly wait to stick a fork in things tomorrow and get STARTED.

DAY 22: THURSDAY

"It's Thanksgiving, Gerald," Mom keeps saying. "Be grateful for what you HAVE."

But all I can think about is what I just LOST. My Flaming Fork!

It was RIGHT THERE on my dresser when I went to bed this morning. But sometime during the day, when everyone else was sleeping, Mom crept around and did one last clean. She took my fork, stuffed it in a cardboard box, and drove it down to the Creeper Charity donation center. NOOOOOO!!!!!

"We HAVE to go get it!" I've been saying ever since I woke up.

But Mom says the fork is long gone. "The truck was pulling away when I got there," she said. "It's halfway to the Nether by now, Gerald." She SURE didn't seem very sorry for what she'd done.

I tried to tell her how much I needed that fork—and how much SHE needed that fork. "I was going to HELP you with Thanksgiving dinner. My Flaming Fork would have made everything taste better. It even made ROTTEN FLESH better," I boasted. "So just think what it would have done for YOUR cooking!"

For some reason, Mom didn't appreciate that comment. She said that Aunt Constance was going to show up ANY minute now, so I'd better "adjust" my attitude.

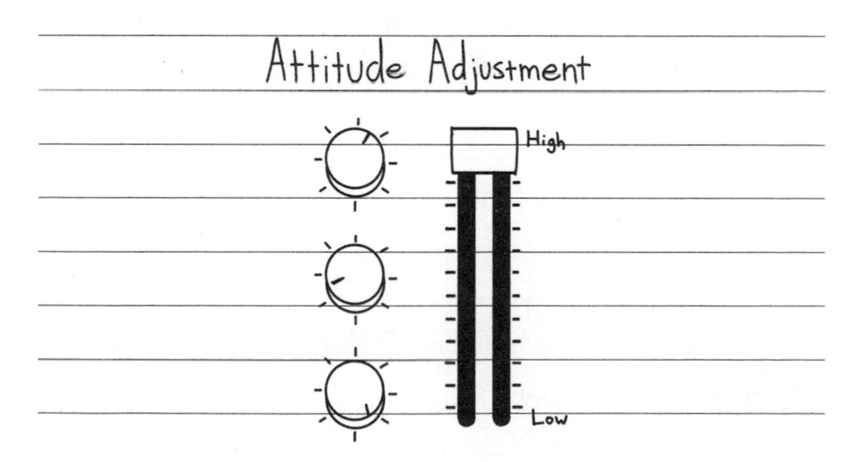

"You can make a new Fire Fork tomorrow," she said.

A WHAT now?

She could at LEAST get the name of my genius invention right. And there was NO WAY I could make another Flaming Fork by tomorrow. I mean, that was the ONLY cool fork in the whole house! And I'd already used my Fire Aspect enchantment. Where was I supposed to get another one?

Ideas flew through my mind like fireballs. Could I . . .

- enchant a book at SCHOOL? Nope. School was closed till Monday.

- FISH for an enchanted book? Not without Willow's lucky pole, and she's not big on sharing with me, I gotta say.

- search for enchanted books in TREASURE CHESTS? Nope. Chests + abandoned mineshafts + cave spiders does NOT equal a good time.

- TRADE for an enchanted book in the nearest human village? Um, NO. We drove through Humanville during a family road trip last summer, and those humans didn't exactly put out their welcome mats for us creepers.

So it turns out, my not-so-genius ideas were more like chicken eggs than fireballs. One by one, they all ended with a CRACK and a SPLAT.

And the doorbell just rang, which means Mom is going to poke her head in here any second now and ask me to set the table—with a bunch of lame little forks that do NOT burn food to a crisp.

So I've got two choices: I've either got to give my attitude an "adjustment," or leap through my open window and head for the hills.

DAY 23: FRIDAY

Well, I didn't run for the hills.

I mean, I WANTED to get out of the house. But then I caught a whiff of roasted potatoes. And it WAS Thanksgiving, after all. So I decided to get a hot meal in my belly before planning my next move.

Now, I'm not gonna lie. The Thanksgiving meal would have been a WHOLE lot better if I'd made it with my Flaming Fork. The potatoes would have been crunchier. The mushroom stew would have been bubblier. The apple crisp would have been crispier.

And those porkchops would have been even more burnt—black as coal.

Dinner also would have been better if Aunt Constance hadn't been looking down her nose at the meal—and at the kitchen, and at every room in our house, and at all of us—since she got here.

No wonder Mom's been prepping for this visit for almost a month. Her big sister is one snooty creeper, with a capital S. Mom kept offering her more food, but Aunt Constance was all like, "I don't think so. I've had quite enough, thank you very much."

I almost felt sorry for Mom, but then I remembered what she'd done with my science project—and I felt MORE sorry for me. Especially when day broke, and we all crept off to bed.

Well, MOST of the family went to bed. Aunt Constance slept in Mom and Dad's bed, because Mom said that one was comfiest. Cate and Chloe slept in Cate's bed, and Mom slept in Chloe's bed. It was like this huge game of musical chairs, except with beds. And guess who got left without a chair—er, a bed?

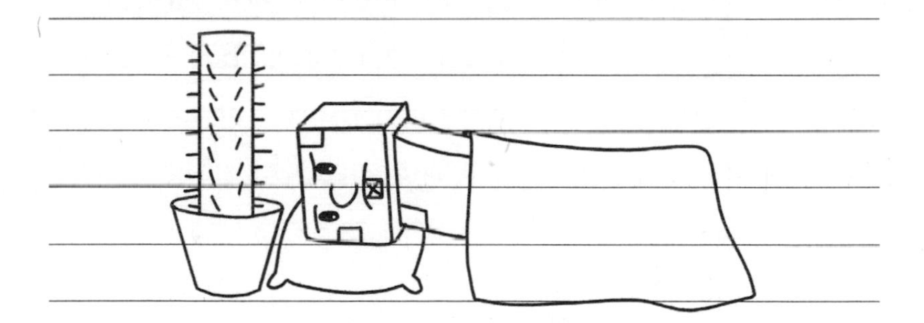

MOI. Gerald Creeper Jr.

Because somehow, Gerald Creeper SENIOR got to sleep in MY bed. And while he was snoring in there, his feet hanging right off the end, I was lying on the cold hard floor of the living room, where a couch USED to be. I told Mom there was NO WAY I could sleep out there, and you know what she said? She said maybe I could use that "awake" time to get some of my homework done.

SERIOUSLY??? Somehow she knows I'm falling behind. Moms have a sixth sense about that stuff.

Well, I didn't exactly dive into my homework, but I did bring a book on enchantments into the living room. I needed ideas for how to make a new Flaming Fork in time for the science fair. But I read that book cover to cover (well, I looked at all the pictures anyway). And I came up with ZERO big ideas.

So I tried to sleep, I really did. But every time I rolled over, I got poked with a cactus needle. That made me think of Sam, bouncing off cacti in his enchanted chest plate. And about the armor he's making for Moo. And about how Willow said I should let Sam use MY anvil for enchanting that armor. Yup, those thoughts popped along, one after another, like minecarts on a track. And guess where that track led?

To an IDEA. Maybe not a genius one, but hey, I've had worse.

I decided to ask Willow if I can borrow her enchanted fishing rod. It's my best chance at getting some enchanted books this weekend. And if the Luck of the Sea enchantment works for ME as well as it worked for her, one of those books MIGHT give me the Fire Aspect enchantment for a new Flaming Fork.

I think Willow will say yes. Why? Because I'm going to BRIBE her with a favor for Sam. If she lets me use her Luck of the Sea enchantment, I'll let Sam use my anvil to make enchanted booties for Moo. That cat will be walking on water in no time.

So now that I have a plan, I'm going to try to catch a few ZZZs. I mean, I HOPE I can catch a few here on the living room floor. But something sharp just poked me in the butt, so . . . it's not looking good.

If you need me, I'll be right here, counting sheep—and cactus prickers.

DAY 25: SUNDAY

So Willow loaned me her fishing rod tonight. She didn't even make a fuss about it, probably because she couldn't care LESS about enchantments. Guess what her science fair project is going to be? An experiment to PROVE that her precious potions are better than enchantments. SHEESH. She just won't let that one go.

Anyway, Sam came fishing with me, but I made him leave Moo at home. I said I wanted to take my dad's old rowboat out to deep water, where I've heard you can find the BEST treasures. And you know, Moo doesn't really swim. (She can't walk on water just yet either—not till Sam enchants those LAME little booties.)

"Doesn't your dad's rowboat have a leak?" Sam asked.

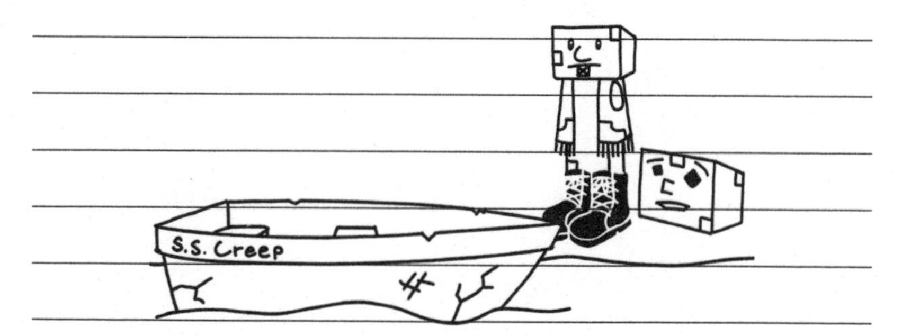

Sometimes I wish that slime didn't have such a good memory.

"Well, YEAH," I said. But I figured we'd catch a few enchanted books before we had to worry about THAT. I mean, Willow's fishing rod was practically glowing with good luck!

By the time we got to the middle of the lake, there was a LITTLE bit of water in our boat. Sam was getting all nervous and jiggly about it, but I said it was no big deal. I mean, the slime lives at the swamp. Is he really worried about getting his feet wet?

Anyway, I cast my line and crossed my own wet toes, hoping for an enchanted book—HOPING for the Fire Aspect enchantment.

And when *that* bobber sunk, tugging at the end of my fishing rod, my heart nearly leaped right out of my chest. I jerked back on the rod, and out *popped* . . . a BOOK! Yes!

I reeled it in and wiped the cover off on my leather vest. Then I read the fine print: CURSE OF BINDING.

Um, curse of WHAT now?

Sam sucked in his breath. I thought he was scared of the curse, but he was actually staring down into the boat, where water was GUSHING in.

What happened next was a total daymare. The boat tilted in Sam's direction. (Big surprise there. I mean, the slime weighs a TON.) And as we plunged into the water, I lost my grip on Willow's fishing rod. I hollered at Sam to grab it, and then I took a deep breath and went under.

This might be a good time to mention that I'm NOT a great swimmer. I mean, I can creep my way through the water. And I was *pretty speedy* with those Depth Strider boots on.

But Sam and I were in deep water now, and I could barely even SEE *the shore*. So I did what any creep would do. I climbed onto my best friend's back and held on for dear life.

Turns out, Sam floats like a *pufferfish*. As I rode *him* like a raft *to shore*, I'd never been more THANKFUL *to have* a slime for a friend. Especially *when* we got to shore and he announced that he'd managed to save IT before we went under.

"The fishing rod?" I asked. Thank GOODNESS. I'd never hear the end of it if I lost Willow's enchanted rod.

But it wasn't the fishing rod. Nope. Sam had saved my enchanted BOOK instead. The one with the curse. The curse that I'm pretty sure just about drowned us.

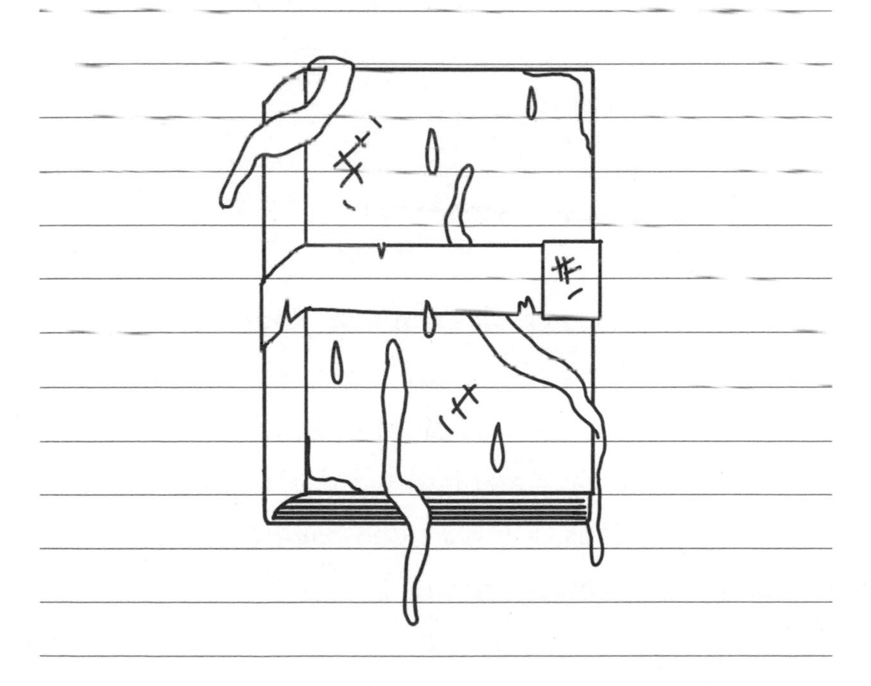

GREAT.

We were supposed to enchant Moo's booties after fishing, but I told Sam I was WAY too wet and freaked out to do any enchanting tonight. And when I read up on the Curse of Binding at home, I got even MORE freaked out.

I guess when you enchant something with the Curse of Binding, you can NEVER let go of that thing. Not EVER—at least not until the thing breaks. Or you die. Whichever comes first.

What kind of a lousy enchantment is THAT???

I threw the book on a shelf in the garage and cursed my own terrible luck. I mean, the science fair is on Friday—five days from now. I don't have a project. I don't have any ideas. I don't have time to come UP with ideas. I don't even have time to get my REGULAR homework done.

And you know what else? I still don't have a BED to sleep in. I guess Aunt Constance has decided to stay a few extra days. GREAT.

Mom doesn't seem very happy about that, either. Maybe it's because Aunt Constance keeps making snippy comments, like how SMALL the house is, and how DRAFTY it seems with the windows open, and how there's nowhere to SIT in the living room, and how it's weird to have a SHEEP in the backyard.

"You can go back to your OWN place anytime," I want to remind her. But kids aren't allowed to say things like *that*.

So I'm *trying* to keep my *trap shut*. I'm actually DYING *to* go back *to* school *tomorrow*—even *though* my homework's not done. Because maybe, just MAYBE, I can enchant a book with Fire Aspect tomorrow in Enchantment Class.

It's my only *hope* of *getting that* jukebox now.

And a creeper's gotta hang on to something, right?

DAY 27: TUESDAY

You know, I don't think I've been giving Ziggy Zombie the respect he deserves. Turns out, I may still have a shot at winning the science fair, and I have ZIGGY to thank for it.

See, I went to school last night hoping to enchant a book with Fire Aspect in Enchantment Class. But that didn't really pan out, because Mrs. Collins picked THAT class to start teaching us about anvils. We didn't even USE the enchantment table!

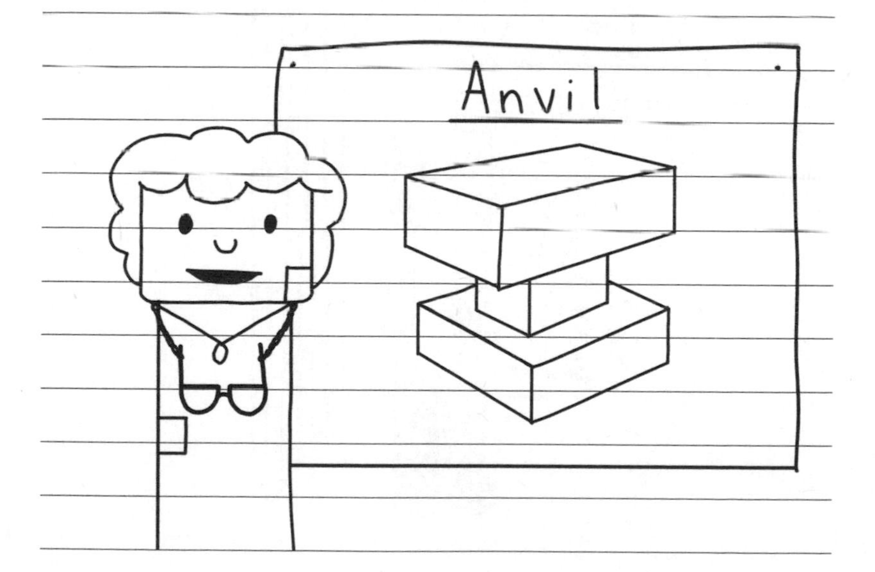

While other kids oohed and aahed over the anvil, I stared longingly at the books on the shelves. If only I could enchant every single one. I'd get the Fire Aspect enchantment for sure! Then I could march right home and enchant a fork—any old fork would do right now.

Sam kept nudging me, asking when we were going to use MY anvil to enchant Moo's booties. "The science fair is FRIDAY," he said. But he didn't have to remind me. That fair was all I could think about.

On the way home from school, I told Sam that if I could JUST get that Fire Aspect enchantment, I'd finish up my project—and be able to help him with his.

We'd been taking the longer, safer way home ever since Bones and his gang of rattlers had started using us for target practice. We walked ALL the way around the running track, where Ziggy Zombie was usually jogging or limping or squatting, checking out his blisters.

So this morning, Ziggy overheard us talking about the Fire Aspect enchantment. And he looked up and said, "Why don't you trade for an enchanted book in the village?"

Ziggy is the only mob I know who goes to the village like ALL the time. He loves scaring villagers, especially at Halloween. He probably still had a bunch of Jack o' Lanterns rotting at home, left over from his favorite holiday.

Anyway, I told Ziggy that I wasn't a big fan of going to the village. And he said, "Why not? I'll go with you!"

Well, normally I would have shot that offer right down. I mean, I like Ziggy and all, but I try not to hang out with him TOO much. The blisters and rashes and rotten-flesh sandwiches kind of get to me, if you know what I mean.

But this morning, I actually said MAYBE I would go. I NEED that enchanted book. And Ziggy said that in the village, you can actually choose the book with the EXACT enchantment you want—if you have enough emeralds, that is.

I told Ziggy I had to go check my piggybank.

Then I asked if he could go with me to the village today. I mean, there's no time like the present, right? And since I was sleeping in the living room these days, it'd be easy for me to sneak out. No one would even know I was gone.

But I'd forgotten something: zombies can't be out in the daylight. I guess the sun burns their skin. And THAT's when I had one of my big ideas—a way to go to the village with Ziggy today, get my enchanted book, and have my new Flaming Fork by TONIGHT.

So Ziggy is going to meet me in the garage in an hour. Why? Because I told him I'd make him an enchanted helmet to protect him from sunlight. I know—genius, right? I'd supply the enchantment of Protection if HE supplied the helmet.

So now I can hardly wait for my family to go to bed. I can't WAIT to stretch out on that cold, hard living room floor. Because as soon as the sun peeks over the horizon, I'm heading to the village. I'm going to get that Fire Aspect enchantment, and get back on track for the science fair.

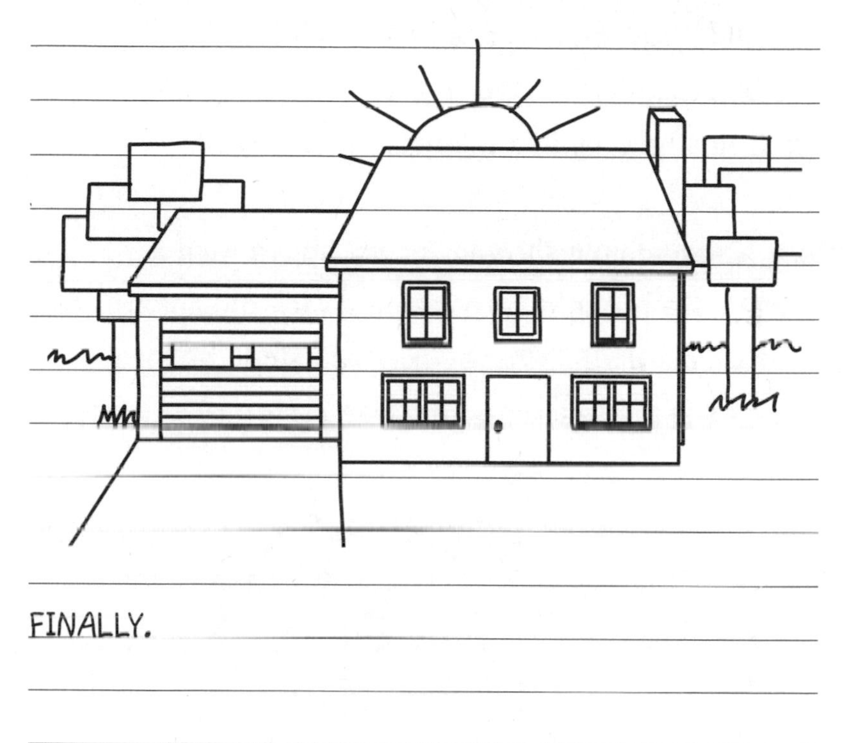

FINALLY.

DAY 27: TUESDAY (CONTINUED)

I should KNOW better than to listen to Ziggy Zombie. Like EVER. Because I did, just this ONE time. And now my life is *pretty* much OVER.

See, Ziggy didn't show up at my house with a helmet. He brought a rotten old Jack o' Lantern. To wear on his HEAD. Whatever. I've said it before—zombies are disgusting. Why was I even surprised?

So I stuck the *pumpkin* in the anvil to give it the Protection enchantment. But the moment the anvil finished doing its clinking thing, my Evil Twin burst through the garage door. And she had Spence the Dispenser with her.

I THOUGHT she'd aim for Ziggy, who didn't happen to be wearing any chicken-egg-deflecting armor. But she didn't. Nope.

She pointed that dispenser at MY face. So I did the only thing I could do. I stuck my head in the freshly enchanted Jack o' Lantern helmet.

Well, I regretted that move RIGHT away. Rotten pumpkins smell even worse than rotten flesh, and pumpkin slime was OOZING down my cheeks. When some of it got in my mouth, I tugged on the pumpkin to get it OFF.

But guess what? It was STUCK.

While Ziggy tried to help me out of that disgusting thing, Chloe cackled in the background. "CURSE OF BINDING!" she cried.

WHAT???

Yup. Somehow, I'd grabbed the wrong book and used the WRONG enchantment. I blame it on Ziggy for distracting me with his stinky Jack o' Lantern. And now that stinky, slimy thing is stuck to my head. Permanently.

FOR LIFE.

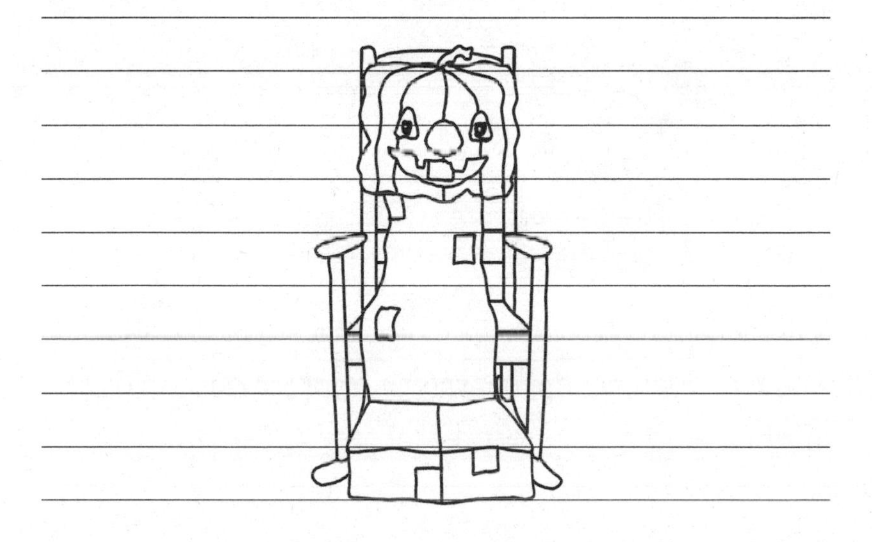

Mom and Dad SAY they'll find a way to get it off. I guess they're going to call Mrs. Collins, even though it's the middle of the day.

But in the meantime? I'm looking at life through two soggy wet holes. I can't breathe through my mouth, or I'll hurl. And even my buddy Sticky the Squid is afraid to look at me.

I've just read my enchantment book cover to cover AGAIN. And when I closed that book, I closed the book on HOPE, too.

Why? Because there's not a SINGLE enchantment in there that can save me now.

DAY 28: WEDNESDAY

Let's just say that I did NOT go to school last night. Oh, I had daymares about it during the few seconds that I actually SLEPT yesterday.

I could picture Bones and his buddies using my HEAD for target practice. And Mrs. Collins using me as an example of what NOT to do with enchantments. And Ziggy Zombie following me around, wishing that rotten vegetable was stuck to HIS head instead of mine.

I guess the only good thing that came out of this stinky situation is that I got my room back. Dad said he'd sleep in the garage from now on.

Did he really JOKE about that? Yes, he did.

But Mom shot him the stink-eye. And when Aunt Constance said that Mom should have kept a better eye on what I was doing out there in the garage, Mom shut her right down. I don't know WHAT she said, but I'm pretty sure I hear Aunt Constance packing in the bedroom next door.

So now I'm just waiting for time to pass—till school ends, when Mrs. Collins is supposed to help us figure this thing out. But I'm not holding my breath. No, I'll probably be locked up in this bedroom for the rest of my life. I've already started marking the hours on my bedroom wall.

1:17 A.M.

Mom just poked her head in and said I should try to keep up on homework. But WHY? Pumpkin Heads don't need an education. I'll probably just join the circus or something—people will pay a LOT of emeralds to go behind the curtain and see a freak like me.

2:05 A.M.

Jukeboxes? Science fairs? I don't care. I can barely HEAR music through my pumpkin helmet anyway.

Kid Z's rap music—my one true love. Lost FOREVER.

3:38 A.M.

I just caught sight of my reflection in Sticky's aquarium, and I'm not gonna lie—I am one SCARY-looking dude. So if Mom wants to take all the mirrors and other shiny things out of the house and donate them to the Creeper Charity, that's fine by me.

4:02 A.M.

True confessions: I just tried on EVERY SINGLE wig and hat in Cate's closet, trying to cover up my orange, bald head. I might have even tried some makeup (but if you tell anyone, I'll deny it).

What's the use??? A pumpkin head is a pumpkin head.

It's such a shame, too. I was a pretty cute creeper, if I do say so myself. But now? I'll NEVER be loved again.

This is NOT a tear. It's a drop of stinky, rotten, pumpkin juice.

4:13 A.M.

I guess there's only one thing left to do.

I mean, I can't study. It's hard to read when you have pumpkin slime oozing into your eyeballs.

I can't see my friends. (Or at least I REALLY don't want them to see ME.)

I can't listen to Kid Z's rap music (cause of my pinched ears. I feel like Sam in his way-too-tight helmet).

I can't eat (because, you know, *pretty much* everything tastes like rotten pumpkin).

So what's left in this world for a Pumpkin Head like me?

Only ONE thing.

SIGH.

So here goes nothing.

DAY 28: WEDNESDAY (CONTINUED)

Okay, I might have gone over to the dark side for a few hours there. And I guess I CAN be kind of dramatic.

But I gotta say, I wrote some pretty great rap songs this morning while I was waiting for the sun to come up. Not for Language Arts. Not for homework. Just for ME.

And it turns out, there WAS an enchantment that could save me from living out my life as a Pumpkin Head. PHEW!!!

When Mrs. Collins called Mom after school this morning, she said to try Silk Touch. "The Jack o' Lantern will fall right off your head," she said. "I mean, probably."

PROBABLY? I wasn't loving the sound of that. I also wasn't thrilled that the only mob I knew who had the Silk Touch enchantment was Willow Witch.

When I called Sam, he bounced right over to the swamp to get her. And I'm pretty sure she used her potion of swiftness, because she and Sam showed up on my doorstep in no time flat. With Moo.

REALLY? Can that slime go NOWHERE without his cat?

Willow brought her Silk Touch pickaxe, which looked awfully sharp. "Just do it," I said, squeezing my eyes shut. I might have said a prayer inside that pumpkin helmet, too.

But Willow wouldn't take the Jack o' Lantern off my head just yet—not until I helped Sam enchant Moo's booties. REALLY???

"A deal's a deal," she said. Like I told you, the witch is fierce when it comes to protecting her boy, Sam.

Let me also say that it's NOT easy to work an anvil when you're stuck inside a pumpkin head. And when EVERYONE in your family is watching you. Chloe was still laughing her butt off, but Cate just stared at my pumpkin head.

"Can you use the Curse of Binding with a WIG?" she asked. Leave it to the Fashion Queen to want a wig stuck to her head for life.

Even Aunt Constance was out in the garage watching me. Wasn't that creeper supposed to be creeping her way back to her own house by now? I'm sure she was feeling all smug, like "None of MY children ever got their heads stuck in a *pumpkin*." Whatever. I didn't have time to worry about her right now.

Willow gave me her enchanted book—the one with Frost Walker. We stuck it in one anvil slot, and we stuck Moo's booties in the other. *Clank, clank, clank.* When the booties started to glow, Sam cheered. He and Moo finally had their "en-CAT-ed" armor.

"Okay, then," I said, turning back toward Willow. "My turn."

But before she could even TOUCH my helmet with her pickaxe, I caught sight of Moo wearing her booties. And let me tell you, that cat looked

RIDICULOUS. She kept shaking her paws, trying to get out of those booties. That poor kitty cat was DANCING.

Well, that tickled my funny bone. I started laughing, which a creep really shouldn't do when he's wearing a pumpkin head. (I snorted a slimy seed up my nose, and it's STILL stuck in there, I swear.)

Anyway, I laughed so hard, I threw my head backward. And thunked the Jack o' Lantern against the wall. And CRACKED it right in half.

HURRAH!!!

When that slimy helmet fell off, my head felt so LIGHT and so FREE. I almost hugged Sam. I could have KISSED Moo, too. But I controlled myself. I mean, this cat-hating creeper has a reputation to protect.

But I wouldn't be protecting it with an ENCHANTMENT anytime soon. Nope, I was kind of done with that anvil for a while. In fact, I'm feeling kind of done with EVERYTHING. There's nothing like a night spent alone with a pumpkin on your head to help you see life more clearly.

So after everyone went home—including Aunt Constance—and the rest of my family went to bed, Mom and I sat on the living room floor and had a good heart to heart.

"I'm cutting the clutter," I told Mom. "No science fair. No more enchantments in the garage. No more worrying about Chloe's dispenser or winning emeralds or getting a jukebox. From now on, it's just me and my rap songs."

"And your homework," said Mom, giving me THAT look. (You know the one.)

I told Mom that I was finally feeling that "positive energy" she kept talking about. "Cutting the clutter feels GREAT."

She smiled, but then she looked around the empty living room and sighed. "I miss the rocking chair," she said.

REALLY? Now she wanted to start putting clutter back IN?

But I've been lying in bed thinking about that, and I kind of get it now. I guess Mom's empty living room is kind of like my long, lonely night in a pumpkin head. Sometimes when you have enough time and space, you figure out what's REALLY important to you—what you miss most. For me, it was my rap songs. For Mom, it's her rocking chair.

So I'm thinking that maybe Dad can build her one. I mean, once we get that anvil out of the garage and clear up some space for new things. I'll talk to Dad about it tomorrow.

DAY 29: THURSDAY

So I was feeling GREAT about my decision to drop out of the science fair. That is, until Ziggy Zombie came up to me at lunchtime and presented me with a gift.

It was wrapped in brown paper that must have been a sandwich wrapper once, because it still had moldy cheese stuck to it. GROSS. But a gift is a gift, so I opened it (FAST).

When an enchanted book fell to the floor, I didn't even want to pick it up. Would it have the Curse of Binding? My heart started thumping.

Ziggy picked it up for me and shoved it in my face. "Fire Aspect!" he said. "The one you wanted!"

I guess Ziggy went to the village right before school and got it for me. That was pretty nice—and brave, considering the sun was still out, and he could have gotten a serious sunburn.

"Now you can make your science project!" he said. "The Flaming Fork!"

Chloe was walking by right about then, and she was all like, "Ooh... the Flaming Fork! Guess the competition's back on, eh, Gerald?" I could tell she was loading up her fire dispenser in her mind, just itching to take me on at the science fair.

I took the book from Ziggy, but I didn't take the bait from Chloe. I told her that I wouldn't be doing a science project, thank you very much.

But Sam kept pestering me. "No science project?" he said. "C'mon, Gerald. It'll be fun!"

FUN? I'd fallen for that trick before. See, I once thought that Enchantment Class would be fun, but it turned into a lot of WORK. I thought that an enchanted pencil would be fun, but I'd gotten in trouble for it. I thought breathing underwater would be fun, but I'd practically DROWNED.

I told Sam that the most fun I'd had lately with science projects was watching him try to get those leather booties on Moo. I cracked up again, just thinking about it.

Sam latched right on to that. "So you can help me with Moo tomorrow!" he said. I guess he's bringing a swimming pool with him into the science room to prove that the Frost Walker enchantment can teach cats to like water.

Well, I gotta say—THAT sounded pretty tempting. So I started thinking that maybe I could enter the science fair after all. I mean, just for FUN.

I came home this morning and made a new Flaming Fork. I wish I could say that it's new and improved, but it's not. See, the only extra fork we had in the drawer was one of Cammy's baby forks. Mom HAS to keep extra of those, because Cammy keeps blowing them up.

My enchanted baby fork looks WAY less impressive than my first Flaming Fork. And it's not going to win me any emeralds—or a jukebox. But, it'll get me into the science room so that I can watch Moo "walk on water." Dude, I'd PAY emeralds just to see that!

DAY 30: FRIDAY

So, just in case you're wondering, cats do NOT like water. Not even three inches of water in a swimming pool. Not even when they're wearing Frost Walker booties.

Sam tried—he really did. And Moo might have taken a step or two across that pool, as the water turned to ice beneath her paws. But then she stood still for a second too long, and the ice turned BACK to water. Well, that cat shot out of the swimming pool faster than a fireball out of Chloe's dispenser.

And speaking of Chloe's dispenser, she and I SOMEHOW ended up working together at the fair. See, our science teacher didn't think she should be shooting fireballs inside the classroom. And when I saw that Chloe was about to blow sky high with disappointment, I did something NICE. I reminded her that she could use chicken eggs.

Our science teacher wasn't crazy about THAT idea either. But I told him that they wouldn't be messy, because I had a secret INVENTION that would clean them right up.

Chloe and I begged for some eggs from the cafeteria, and then we showed off her Fried-Egg Machine. She pelted my leather vest with eggs, and I fried them with my Flaming Fork—and served them up to all our friends, including the three judges walking around the room. (Genius, right?)

I steered clear of Ziggy's science poster, which was FULL of blister photos. (YUCK) But I did catch Willow's demonstration. She was testing out some of her potions against enchantments.

Potion of Harming versus Protection Enchantment? Chalk one up for Willow. When she threw her glass bottle at an enchanted shield, that shield cracked right in half.

Fire Protection versus Potion of Fire Resistance? Yup, Willow won again. She stood in a bucket of hot lava while the enchanted boots in the bucket next to hers went up in smoke.

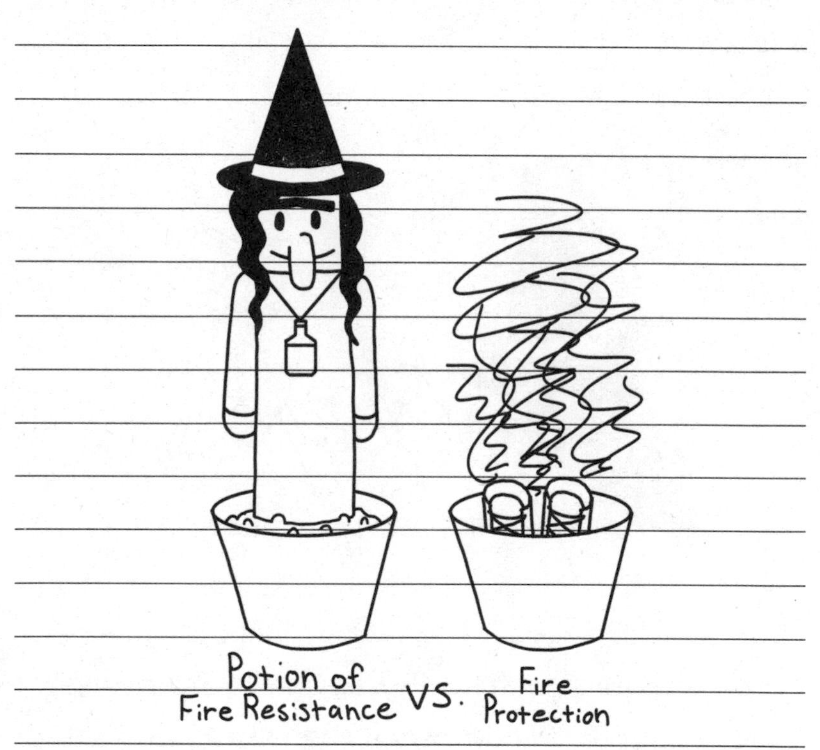

When the judges handed Willow a blue ribbon, I figured it was all over. Willow won the emeralds, and that was okay by me. But you know what happened next? The judges gave ALL of us blue ribbons. Yup, even Ziggy Zombie. I guess they'd decided to do away with a winner and reward us all for having "fun with science."

Chloe was hopping mad about that, and I kind of get it. I mean, like I said: grown-ups know how to take something fun and make it feel like work. Then they'll take something we worked HARD on, and say it was just for fun!

Still, I'm not gonna lie—I DID have fun.

As Sam, Willow, and I walked home after the fair, I congratulated Willow on her potions. "I guess potions are pretty cool after all," I admitted.

"Hey!" said Sam. "We should start a Potions Club!"

Well, Willow and I both shut him down. The last thing I need is ONE MORE ACTIVITY in my schedule. But I told Willow that maybe we could brew potions at her house someday—you know, just for fun.

By the time I got home, Mom had put some furniture back in the living room. She was standing in the doorway with her eyebrows all scrunched up, thinking. "Do you think it looks too cluttered now?" she asked me.

I froze on the spot. UH-OH, I thought. Here we go again.

But when I said no, Mom agreed. Then you know what she did? She went right over to the new couch and curled up for a nap.

I think I'll go to my room, too. But I'm not going to sleep. No, I'm going to do my favorite thing in the whole wide world.

I'm going to RAP.

DON'T MISS ANY OF GERALD CREEPER JR.'S HILARIOUS ADVENTURES!

Sky Pony Press
New York